The truck swerved and smashed into a fire hydrant.

Diving for the side of the road, Alex landed on the hard asphalt.

A large barrel flew out of the back of the truck. It crashed and split open before landing in the street. A gold fluid poured from the broken container and mixed with the water that sprayed from the hydrant.

A sparkling, golden rain drenched Alex from head to toe.

Coughing and sputtering, Alex scrambled to her feet. "Oh, man!" Disgusted by the ooze dripping off her, Alex looked at the broken barrel. Gold fluid oozed out onto the street, but that was not what grabbed her attention. The truck bore the words HAZARDOUS CHEMICAL TRANSPORT.

She had a lot more to worry about than ruined new shoes and an upset mother. She was in trouble.

Big trouble.

The Secret World of Alex Mack™

Available from MINSTREL Books

the secret world of
ALEX MACK™

Alex, You're Glowing!

Diana G. Gallagher

Adapted from a teleplay by Ken Lipman and Thomas W. Lynch

A MINSTREL® BOOK

PUBLISHED BY POCKET BOOKS

New York   London   Toronto   Sydney   Tokyo   Singapore

A MINSTREL PAPERBACK *Original*

A Minstrel Book published by
POCKET BOOKS, a division of Simon & Schuster Inc.
1230 Avenue of the Americas, New York, NY 10020

Copyright © 1995 by Viacom International, Inc., and RHI Entertainment, Inc. All rights reserved. Based on the Nickelodeon series entitled "The Secret World of Alex Mack."

ISBN: 0-671-52599-9

First Minstrel Books printing April 1995

10 9 8 7 6 5 4 3

A MINSTREL BOOK and colophon are registered trademarks of Simon & Schuster Inc.

NICKELODEON and all related titles, logos and characters are trademarks of Viacom International, Inc.

Cover photos by Thomas Queally and Danny Feld

Printed in the U.S.A.

For Nora Clancy,
my friend and teen expert,
with many thanks for her enthusiasm and help

Alex, You're Glowing!

CHAPTER 1

Peeking out from beneath rumpled covers, Alex Mack watched Annie tuck her bedspread under a perfectly centered pillow and smooth out the remaining wrinkles. Not only was her older sister awake and dressed, but her side of the bedroom was neat as a pin, too. Alex's half was a mess.

Neat freak, Alex thought sleepily. It was too early to be so organized, but then Annie had not known a single, disorganized moment in her entire life. Pulling the blanket back over her head, Alex yawned and closed her eyes.

1

"Alex," Annie cooed. "Are you planning to get up?"

Alex tensed. She didn't have to see Annie's face to know the expression of disgust. It matched her superior attitude.

"Alex, you know there's no way Mom will let you sleep through your first day of junior high."

Groaning as she pushed back the blanket, Alex squinted at Annie through bleary eyes.

Annie smiled with exaggerated sweetness. "Yes. Isn't it an exciting day?"

Dragging herself to a sitting position, Alex sighed as Annie walked briskly out of the room. It was either going to be the best or the worst day of her life. For thirteen years she had accepted being ordinary and dull. All that could change today. Junior high. A new start. First impressions were so important . . . and she was wasting time!

Alex jumped out of bed and rummaged through the pile of clothes on the floor, tossing aside wrinkled tops and dirty jeans. She finally threw on a T-shirt and jean shorts, rushed into the hall, and pounded on the bathroom door.

"Come on, Annie, hurry up! I'm completely late already," she shouted.

The door swung open. "This is not a good start, Alex," Annie said, peering over her toothbrush. "Why don't you try to relax a little?"

"How can I relax? My entire life begins today!"

"I'll alert the media." Rinsing thoroughly, then slipping the toothbrush into the holder, Annie squeezed past Alex and headed for the stairs.

Frantic, Alex studied herself in the mirror. Long, dark-blond hair fell in unruly tangles to her shoulders and her large brown eyes were still puffy with sleep. *Hopeless*, Alex thought.

After washing her face, Alex dashed back into the bedroom and slipped on a plaid flannel shirt to complete the ultra-casual look. Then, as she was trying one cap after another and throwing the rejects behind her, her mother's voice drifted up the stairwell from the living room.

"Annie, where's your sister?"

"Upstairs, trying unsuccessfully to redefine herself through fashion," Annie said matter-of-factly.

Too true. Jamming a red baseball cap on back-

3

ward, Alex stared at her reflection. "Face it, Alex. You're boring. Plain and simple. Boring."

Vince, head of security at Paradise Valley Chemical, hurried toward the CEO's office. Blond and athletically trim with icy blue eyes, his stony face bore no trace of humor. *Strictly business,* he thought as he pushed through the heavy security doors leading into Danielle Atron's office.

"You sent for me, Ms. Atron?" Vince walked smartly across the carpet and sat in a chair facing the massive desk. The chief executive officer's office was decorated in black and white with gray chrome. The stark surroundings emphasized the absolute power of the woman who occupied it.

"I was just on the phone with our testing facility," Danielle said from the far side of the room, absently touching an exotic red plant. A handsome woman of forty with dark hair arranged in a twist at the back of her head, she wore a white silk blouse and a tailored dark skirt. Danielle turned and fixed Vince with her direct, no-nonsense gaze. "They'll be ready

4

for the GC One-Sixty-One transport later this afternoon."

"That's good news, Ms. Atron." Vince did not flinch as Danielle circled behind him.

"It has to go smoothly." Pausing at the corner of her desk, Danielle stared down at him to make her point. "You're the only one I can trust for something like this."

Vince nodded modestly, but he was secretly delighted with her praise. The CEO did not trust just anyone, and Vince liked being the only person in the company who had earned her unwavering confidence.

"You won't have to think about it again," Vince assured her.

"I won't." Danielle's hard expression softened. "Vince?"

"Yes?"

"Isn't this an exciting day?"

Vince allowed himself a rare, tight-lipped smile and nodded in agreement. "Yes, it is."

Alex paused at the top of the stairs and took a deep breath. Below, her mother paced in the living room talking into the cordless phone. An account executive at a local public relations firm, Barbara Mack was enthusiastic, energetic, efficient, and always on the go.

Alex listened to the conversation, wishing she felt as confident about junior high as her mother did about her work.

"I'll have to reschedule that lunch for later this week. Make sure I have copies of the market research on my desk when I get in, okay? Let me talk to Judy."

Reminding herself that her friends were facing the first day of junior high, too, Alex started down the stairs. She stopped halfway when she realized Annie was still in the kitchen. Born with their mother's confidence and their father's brains, Annie was never nervous about anything, especially school. Most of the time Alex felt like a total nerd by comparison.

Feeling anxious and inadequate, Alex sat down on the stairs and peered through the railing to watch her brilliant sister.

Annie was in no hurry to leave. Picking up a piece of toast, she wandered to the kitchen table to peer over her father's shoulder.

A color diagram of a complex molecule and

related information filled the small screen of a compact computer sitting on the table in front of George Mack. The image was a total mystery to Alex. Annie, however, was full of curious questions.

"What are you working on, Dad? You haven't taken your eyes off that screen for days."

Mr. Mack, a research and development scientist at Paradise Valley Chemical, stared at the screen as he made another entry. Their dad was often oblivious to the details of daily life going on around him, but he and Annie had a lot in common, especially their shared genius and passion for math and the sciences.

Math and science were Alex's absolutely worst subjects.

Mr. Mack looked up and smiled at Annie. "I'm working on that incredible new compound I was telling you about, GC One-Sixty-One. There's quite a buzz at the plant about it."

"Are you on the mechanism or applications end?" Annie asked.

"Strictly on the mechanism end." Sliding out of his chair, Mr. Mack let Annie take over the keyboard. "Everything else about it is very top secret. I have no idea what they have in mind to do with it, but it has some extraordinary properties.''

Who cares? Sighing, Alex leaned against the railing.

The doorbell rang.

''Annie!'' Mrs. Mack called. ''Get the door, please.''

''It's open!'' Annie shouted, her attention fastened on the computer screen.

Alex smiled as Raymond Alvarado sauntered through the door. Aside from the fact that he had been her best friend for years, his easygoing presence always took the edge off Annie's biting tongue. Taking a deep breath, Alex stood up and walked down the stairs.

Carrying a saxophone case, Raymond greeted Mrs. Mack in passing and ambled into the kitchen.

''Good morning, Raymond.'' Mr. Mack shook Raymond's hand without looking up from the computer screen.

''Hey, Mr. Mack. Where's Alex?''

Annie shot Raymond an annoyed look. ''Going through pretraumatic stress syndrome.''

Alex trudged down the last three steps on feet that felt like lead weights. She couldn't even fake a smile as her mother slipped an arm around her and, phone to ear, steered her into the kitchen.

"Fresh from the pages of *Chaos* Magazine, it's . . . Alex Mack." Annie stared at Alex's outfit and raised an eyebrow. "You've managed to achieve the look that screams disorderly, distressed, and desperate. How appropriate."

Alex looked down at the plaid shirt covering an oversize T-shirt with horizontal blue, red, black, and white stripes and jean shorts accented by rumpled socks and Doc Martens. Then she glanced at Annie, who was wearing a simple, sleeveless blue blouse and plain white pants. If she didn't feel bad before, she felt terrible now.

"I think you look great," Raymond said with an approving nod.

"Really?" Alex appreciated Raymond's interest, but he was wearing baggy pants and an open blue shirt over a white T-shirt with a huge smiley face.

"Lighten up, Alex," Annie said. "You're just starting junior high—not Harvard University."

"You missed breakfast," their mother said.

"That's all right. I'm not hungry." Alex sighed, feeling totally overwhelmed by the prospects of higher education.

"I could eat." Raymond craned his head toward Mrs. Mack and smiled.

Without even a glance, Mrs. Mack handed Raymond a bagel and looked at Alex. "You're just nervous about your first day at a new school. You're going to be just fine."

"Please don't expect me to be the award-winning genius Annie is."

Mrs. Mack smiled reassuringly and brushed Alex's hair back over her shoulder. "Darling, we don't expect you to be like Annie."

"That's true, Alex," Annie said. "In fact, if you just make it to the next grade, they'll be ecstatic."

"Annie, enough." Their mother silenced Annie sternly, then brightened as she turned back to Alex. "I have a surprise for you." Mrs. Mack pulled a pink, plastic lunch box out of a paper bag.

Alex's smile of anticipation became a look of

stunned disbelief. She stared at the lunch box her mother shoved toward her. Cartoon pictures of trolls decorated both sides.

Annie was quick to comment. "Trolls. Very cutting edge, huh, Alex?"

Alex's shoulders drooped, but she managed to smile and mutter. "Thanks, Mom. It's, uh . . . great. Really." Her mother looked so pleased, Alex couldn't reject the geeky gift. Turning, she slipped the lunch box into her large backpack.

Raymond was more enthusiastic. "Extremely cool. Trolls are so retro."

Alex caught Raymond's eye as he shrugged and grinned. He was sincerely trying to make her feel better and she did—a little. Raymond always made her see the lighter side of any situation.

"Guess we'd better get going," she said.

Mrs. Mack turned to her husband. "George? Don't you have something to say to Alex before her first day of junior high school?"

Mr. Mack did not hear her.

Annie tapped him gently on the shoulder. "Dad . . ."

"Huh? Oh, yes, well . . ." Rising slowly, Mr.

Mack walked over to Alex and paused. "Well, Alex . . . um . . . well. Good luck." He gave her an awkward hug.

"Thanks, Dad. Come on, Ray." Alex rushed out of the kitchen, anxious to get the first day of junior high over with.

CHAPTER 2

Dressed in a yellow environmental suit, Vince watched as a gray, high-tech truck backed into the secured loading dock. A wide blue stripe was painted on the side with the words: HAZARD-OUS CHEMICAL TRANSPORT. Inside the cab, the driver flipped a switch and the truck's heavy back door unlocked and opened. The interior was filled with a yellow mist.

Ordinarily, Vince did not personally supervise the handling and shipment of cargo. However, GC 161 was Danielle Atron's prized project and heads would roll if anything went wrong. The transfer operation would be completed without a hitch, Vince decided with single-minded determination. The CEO's respect and Vince's reputation depended on it.

As two men wearing identical protective gear joined him, Vince slid his coded badge into a locking device. The corrugated steel door leading into an area marked AUTHORIZED PERSONNEL ONLY rolled upward. Vince walked ahead down a short corridor to another security door. Punching numbers into a wall panel, he waited until the handprint ID board activated. Removing his glove, he put his hand on the panel and was instantly recognized.

CLASSIFIED ACCESS GRANTED.

Vince led the way down a longer hallway. A set of thick, towering doors swung outward to let them pass through. Inside the priority storage area, three large yellow barrels waited in an orderly row. The plant logo, a large letter C with a hand holding a test tube nested inside, was stenciled on each container.

The three men grabbed the handles of the dollies that were already in place underneath the barrels. In unison, they lifted the containers off the floor, wheeled them around, and carefully pushed the valuable cargo toward the corridor.

Vince tensed as the huge doors thundered closed. Being in charge of security at Paradise Valley Chemical was a serious business that required clear thinking and total dedication. Neither he nor Danielle Atron had ever doubted his qualifications, but he had never handled an operation as dangerous and important as the transfer of GC 161.

He watched every move as the cargo handlers loaded and secured the barrels inside the truck. Nothing would go wrong.

As they walked, Alex listened to Raymond's excited chatter with mounting anxiety. Ray couldn't wait to enter the hallowed halls of Danielle Atron Junior High. Alex wanted to drop off the face of the Earth and forget everything.

"Junior high!" Raymond spun in a complete circle as he walked. "It's about time."

"I feel like I'm on a death march to my final resting place." Alex trudged up the stairs of the bridge that spanned the four-lane highway.

Alex wasn't sure why she was so worried. Everyone from her old sixth-grade class would be in the seventh grade with her. She was especially eager to see Robyn and Nicole. Both girls had been on vacation for the last few weeks, and Alex had missed them.

Red-headed, with pale skin that got sunburned easily, Robyn was smart, but she had a depressingly realistic attitude toward everything. If something could go wrong, Robyn was certain that it would. Nicole was outspoken, passionate, and fearless. She did not flinch from a justified fight and was a dedicated defender of the rights of everyone and everything . . . even trees.

When they reached the top of the stairs, Alex paused to look out over Paradise Valley. The town lay to the west of the four-lane highway below. The chemical plant, where her father and half the population of Paradise Valley worked, was located in an isolated area to the south. Remodeling the quaint town had been Danielle Atron's first community service after she had become the CEO of Paradise Valley Chemical.

"Come on, Alex!" Raymond stopped a few steps ahead. "It's still just school."

"Just school?" Alex caught up and gave Raymond a quizzical look. It wasn't just school. Junior high was completely new and unknown territory. Junior high meant changing classes, getting from one room to another on time, and having several teachers to please. Junior high meant more responsibility, more homework, harder tests, and dealing with a hundred other seventh graders rather than thirty classmates bound together because they were assigned to one room with the same teacher. And now they were at the bottom of the heap under eighth and ninth graders who had the advantage of one or two more years of valuable experience.

"The way I see junior high," Raymond went on, "is that there's no more monkey bars. The stakes are bigger now. The work's harder, the girls are prettier. It's time to sink or swim—and I'm a shark!"

Boys! Alex's heart lurched. They weren't little kids anymore. They were teenagers facing dances and dates, clubs and cliques, popularity or anonymity, success or failure. Junior high *is* a whole new ball game with a new set of rules.

Alex stopped suddenly. So did Raymond.

They both stared. Below them stood Danielle Atron Junior High School, a sprawling collection of classrooms, teachers, and students—intimidating, yet just a bit exciting and full of promise. Here she'd have the chance to redefine herself, to rise above the boring, average image of her past.

It's sink or swim for me, too, Alex thought with renewed determination. *Junior high is just school, like Raymond said. I can handle it if I just stay calm and cool. Nothing to worry about.*

Still, Alex shivered in the morning sun as she followed Ray down the far side of the bridge and toward the front doors.

With her schedule clutched in one hand, Alex walked down the main corridor through a sea of talking, laughing, bustling teenagers. The hall was packed. There was no sign of Nicole, but she finally found Robyn.

"I saw Nicole a few minutes ago," Robyn said as she fumbled with the numbered dial on a locker. "We're in the same science class fifth period."

Alex scanned her schedule. "With Mr. Krantz?"

Robyn nodded, then glowered at the lock. She began twirling it again, muttering the combination aloud. "Left to fourteen. Right to three. Left to twenty-one . . ."

"I've got fifth period science with Krantz, too!" Alex grinned. Knowing she'd be in at least one class with her friends took some of the edge off the day.

"They gave me the wrong combination." Robyn scowled at the yellow paper in her hand. "It figures."

"Here, let me try." Glancing at the numbers, Alex turned the dial. "I don't even know where my locker is."

"Don't waste your time, Alex. With my luck, it's probably not the right combination—not for *this* locker anyway. I'd better run. See you later."

Stopping the arrow on twenty-one exactly, Alex turned the handle and the locker door swung open. Too late. Robyn had already disappeared into the crowd. Shrugging, Alex closed the door and set out to find her first period class.

Swept along by the mass of bodies, Alex gazed at room numbers, trying to figure out where she was supposed to be. She was not looking where she was going, and she collided with a large man.

Startled, Alex swallowed a cry of alarm. She watched in horror as the man stumbled backward, flailing his arms to keep from falling through a door that suddenly opened behind him. He caught himself by gripping both sides of the doorjamb. The surprised boy behind him ducked back into the classroom. He let go of the door and it swung closed—on the man's fingers.

"Oh, I'm so sorry!" Alex gasped.

The man straightened and shook his stinging fingers. Fixing her with a stern gaze, he quickly recovered his dignity. "I am Vice Principal Heller," he barked. "Who, may I ask, are you?"

"Alex Mack, sir. I, uh—" Her voice froze in her throat as Mr. Heller leaned toward her, his hands on his hips.

"I suggest you pay a little more attention to where you're going, young lady. Before someone gets hurt."

"Yes, sir," Alex mumbled.

As the vice principal marched away, another wave of students caught her unaware. Shoved aside by a passing shoulder, Alex fell against the wall and dropped her schedule. She waited until most of the human tide had passed, then stooped to pick up the paper.

As Alex reached for the schedule, a sneaker landed on it. Her hand closed on the corner, and she heard a ripping sound. She looked at the torn piece in her hand, blinked, then picked up the other half.

Five minutes later, she finally found her math class. She was ten minutes late.

Hoping to sneak into the room without drawing too much attention to herself, Alex carefully turned the doorknob.

"So we'll start with a little review. I assume you've all covered this basic territory in your sixth grade classes . . ." The teacher was writing on the blackboard with her back turned.

Alex's bad luck held firm. As she opened the door, a hinge squeaked. The teacher stopped talking in midsentence. Every head in the room turned to gawk as Alex stood in the open doorway. Although she saw a couple of familiar faces, she didn't actually know anyone in the room. None of them had been in Mrs. Judd's sixth-grade class or lived in her neighborhood.

Under the teacher's disapproving gaze, Alex slid into an empty seat. She ignored the snickers of her classmates and was grateful when the teacher, deciding not to say anything about her tardiness, turned back to the blackboard.

A wad of paper hit Alex in the back of the neck. Stifled giggles rose around her.

"Class, please—settle down. Now where was I?" The teacher paused. "Oh, of course. The basic principles of algebra."

Alex silently vowed to get through the rest of the day without anything else going wrong. Her first half hour of junior high had certainly not been boring, but being tagged as a major dweeb by the vice principal and the other kids was not exactly the first impression she had had in mind.

The teacher continued talking. "If AX squared plus BX plus C equals zero, then X equals minus B plus or minus the square root of B squared minus four AC over . . . what?"

Alex picked up her class schedule and pretended to study it. Around her, the other students frantically waved their hands. She didn't dare volunteer. Without Annie's help, she'd never have gotten the hang of long division

in the third grade. Algebra was completely beyond her.

The teacher turned to a class list lying on the
desk and picked a name at random. "Alexandra Mack."

Alex's heart sank as expectant faces looked
around in anticipation of the answer.

She didn't have a clue.

CHAPTER 3

Vince strode across the parking lot and stopped in front of Dave. The driver was sitting on the pavement, leaning against the wall of the building with his eyes closed. He did not seem to realize that the head of plant security was standing in front of him.

"You're the best we've got?" Vince asked sharply.

Dave slowly opened his eyes and shrugged. "Most of the other guys are out on runs."

Vince stared at Dave's unconcerned face, making a mental note to yell at the person in charge of scheduling drivers. So far, everything about the secret transfer of GC 161 to the testing facility had gone without a hitch. Now, suddenly, Vince was worried.

"You ready to roll or what?" Vince snapped, but the angry warning in his clipped tone didn't faze the relaxed driver.

"You mind if I grab some lunch on the way?" Dave glanced at Vince.

Vince held Dave's untroubled gaze with his own steely stare. "This is important! Your lunch can wait." He tossed Dave the keys to the truck. "And take back roads—no stopping, no nothing. Do you understand?" Vince asked through clenched teeth.

Dave hesitated with a puzzled frown. "Which part?"

Vince checked a surge of fury and clasped his hands behind his back. The secret cargo had to be delivered according to Danielle Atron's schedule. He had no choice but to let Dave drive. Nobody else was available. Vince sighed and tried not to imagine all the things that could go wrong.

* * *

When the final bell rang, Alex burst through the front doors feeling as though she had just awakened from the most horrible nightmare of her life.

Raymond was waiting for her outside. "Hey, Alex!"

"Hi, Ray," Alex mumbled as she fell into step beside him.

"You're looking kinda down, Alex. What's the problem?"

Pausing, Alex gazed past him as she tried to collect her thoughts. Several older girls were playing basketball on a nearby court, laughing and cheering each other on. A trim, pretty girl with a long ponytail made a perfect jump shot, then slapped a teammate's upraised hand in victory.

"Way to go, Jessica!" a boy shouted from the sidelines. "The Green Fields team doesn't stand a chance against you guys!"

Alex watched Jessica wistfully. Not only was she a good basketball player, she was confident and totally accepted by everyone. Pretty, poised, and popular, there was nothing ordinary abut her. She was everything Alex wanted to be.

The few friends Alex had were good friends, and she wouldn't trade them for anything, but outside that small circle, her name was unknown. She was a pathetic athlete and a less than brilliant student. Rising to junior high stardom on the newspaper or in sports was an impossible dream. Nothing about her was even remotely remarkable. *Maybe*, Alex thought glumly, *there isn't any escape from being hopelessly average*.

"Hey, Alex. What's the matter?"

"I can't believe it, Ray. It's worse than I thought it would be. I was shoved in a locker, my schedule got ripped in half, and everyone here hates me—including Vice Principal Heller."

"I like you," Ray said sincerely.

"No offense, Ray, but I'll need more than you to survive here. I'd say I'm sinking. Let's just go home."

"No can do. Band tryouts."

"Band tryouts." Alex looked at him in disbelief. "You're gonna join the band?"

Raymond shrugged, raising the saxophone case. "I have to try. You know my dad. The Alvarados have a history of playing in school bands, and I can't break the tradition." His dark eyes sparkled suddenly. "Besides, maybe I'll meet some girls."

"I'm a girl."

"Girl-type girls, Alex," Raymond said pointedly.

"Oh, girl-type girls." Alex felt crushed. It wasn't that she had any interest in Raymond beyond the friendship they already had. It was just that not even he thought of her as anyone but plain, old, ordinary Alex Mack.

"I'll come over later," Raymond promised as he turned and headed back toward the school.

"Okay." Alex continued on alone across the lawn. She stared at the ground, lost in her own depressing thoughts.

"Hey—get out of the way!"

The warning came too late. Alex found herself crashing into one of the basketball players. The impact sent her sprawling on the ground and her backpack flying. Books and pencils, papers, and the pink, plastic lunch box scattered on the ground around her. Dazed, Alex looked up at the girl hovering over her.

"Why don't you watch where you're going!" Jessica was livid with anger.

Numb and speechless, Alex sat motionless in the middle of the court. Jessica glared at her for a long moment. Alex looked away and groaned. As if things weren't bad enough, her pink troll lunch box was lying at Jessica's feet.

Following Alex's mortified gaze, Jessica laughed. "Yo, Ellen! Guys! Check out this lunch box."

"What's so funny?" A tall, attractive girl stepped up beside her teammate. She rolled her eyes and giggled when she saw the pink lunch box. "Trolls? Toooo much! You've *got* to be kidding!"

Several other members of the team formed a semicircle in front of Alex and began laughing and pointing. Alex wished she could melt into the ground.

Grabbing the lunch box and her other things, Alex shoved them into the backpack without looking up. All she wanted to do was get out of there as fast as possible.

Beyond the crowd standing around her, another girl heaved the basketball in her direction. Alex saw the rocketing ball out of the corner of her eye and ducked. The defensive move was unnecessary. A foot suddenly appeared out of nowhere and kicked the basketball aside before it hit her.

"What are you guys doing to her?"

Alex's heart fluttered as she glanced up and saw the boy who had spoken. Handsome, with short brown hair and brown eyes, he was completely hot. And he had come to her rescue!

"Man, Scott, relax," Jessica said. "We're just messing around."

Scott. Alex could only stare at him. He was just the cutest guy she'd ever seen.

"Chill out, Jessica." Scott waved toward the hoop on the far side of the court. "Go back to practice."

Frowning, Jessica hesitated. When Scott insisted with a determined look, she exhaled in exasperation and motioned the other girls to follow.

"First day?"

"Huh?" Alex started, then stared at the hand Scott held out to her. She took it and managed a weak nod as she rose on unsteady legs.

"It'll get better," Scott assured her with a warm smile.

"I hope so." Alex shifted her weight self-consciously.

Scott picked up her backpack and handed it to her. "What's your name?"

"Alex." Slinging the bag over her shoulder, she smiled slightly. "Uh, Alexandra."

"Hey, Scott!" Jessica yelled. "Why don't you ask her about trolls? She's an expert!"

The other girls laughed, then resumed their play.

Scott glanced toward Jessica, then frowned uncertainly at Alex. "What? You like trolls or something?"

Alex's heart pounded against her ribs, and she wondered if Scott had seen the pink lunch box. "Uh, I used to, but not now. I mean, not anymore . . ."

Scott was watching her and listening with disarming intensity.

Get a grip! Alex said to herself. She couldn't let Scott leave thinking she was a complete dork. She'd never be able to face him again. "I'm too old for troll dolls . . . any dolls . . ." Her voice trailed off as Scott smiled and backed away.

"Well, uh . . . see ya."

31

Alex watched him go, her spirits sinking even lower as she hurried toward the street. *I'm completely and utterly hopeless,* she thought. With luck, Scott wouldn't even recognize her tomorrow. *Better to be forgotten than remembered as a stupid geek.*

Dave wasn't worried about Vince being angry at him. He would throw away all the evidence of the late lunch he had bought at a drive-thru before he got back to the chemical plant. Vince would never know.

Eating the sandwich without spilling the soda while trying to steer was a problem, though. And he was running behind schedule because he had stopped.

Pressing his foot on the gas, Dave struggled to unwrap a deluxe sandwich and almost dumped the drink. That would not be good. Vince would notice sticky soda stains on the seat, and Vince would not be happy if he found out Dave had disobeyed a direct order. He could lose his job.

The truck jolted over a bump, and Dave's hand tightened around the paper cup. Soda squished out from the small hole in the plastic lid. *Gotta get rid of the drink,* Dave decided.

As he reached to set the drink on the dashboard, his hand hit the switch that controlled the back doors. Dave frowned at the device. What was that for again? And what was that banging noise?

About to miss his turn, Dave forgot the noise and jerked the steering wheel around. The truck roared around the corner on screeching tires.

Immersed in frustration and self-pity, Alex stepped off the curb without looking and headed across the street. The squeal of tires on pavement barely broke through her daze.

Confused for a moment, Alex stopped dead in the middle of the street. She turned and froze as a truck sped toward her on a collision course.

CHAPTER 4

The speeding truck came straight at her.

Paralyzed with fear, Alex stared through the windshield at the driver's panicked face. For seconds that seemed suspended in time, she stood in the middle of the street.

Move or you're dead! The thought screamed in her mind.

Alex ran.

The driver hit the brakes.

Diving for the side of the road, Alex landed on the hard asphalt. A sharp pain shot through her arm, and air *whooshed* from her lungs.

The truck swerved, jumped the curb, and smashed into a fire hydrant.

A large barrel flew out of the back of the truck. It crashed against the truck's hard bumper, and split open before it landed in the street. A gold fluid poured from the broken container and mixed with the water that sprayed from the hydrant.

A sparkling, golden rain drenched Alex from head to toe.

Coughing and sputtering, Alex scrambled to her feet. "Oh, man!" Disgusted by the ooze dripping off her, Alex stared at her golden hands and sleeves, then down at her new Doc Martens. The gold stuff had soaked them through. *Mom is going to kill me!*

"Why don't you watch where you're going?" The angry driver waved a fist at her.

Alex looked at the broken barrel. Gold fluid oozed out onto the street, but that was not what grabbed her attention. The Paradise Valley Chemical Plant logo was stenciled on the side of the barrel, and the truck bore the words HAZ-ARDOUS CHEMICAL TRANSPORT. She had a lot more to worry about than ruined new shoes and an upset mother. She was in trouble. Big trouble.

Executing an about-face, Alex jumped out of the street. Water from the broken hydrant drenched the ground of the vacant lot. Alex slipped in the mud and lost her balance. She saved herself from falling facedown in the brown goo with her outstretched hands, then scrambled to her feet and ran.

"Hey, kid! Get over here!"

Alex glanced back for a second to see if the driver was chasing her. He wasn't. He was looking at the mess on the street. Then he threw his hat on the ground.

Alex did not hang around to see what he would do next. Soaked to the skin with nasty gold gunk, she bolted for home.

Scared and exhausted, Alex hid in the bushes outside the house and crept past the kitchen window to avoid running into her mother. Her skin itched and her arms and legs tingled with a growing heat. *Hazardous chemical.* The warning painted on the barrel haunted her. She just knew the mysterious gold gunk had done something awful to her, and she really didn't need a lecture about taking better care of her things or tracking sticky gold stuff over the clean floors and carpets.

Dashing to the garage, she pounded on the large doors.

"Annie? Annie!" Alex called. No answer. Her sister was not home yet, Alex figured. Otherwise she'd be in the garage that served as laundry room, storage area, and lab for her many experiments.

Trying not to panic, Alex entered the dim garage and dropped her wet bag on the washer. She dashed to the sink, turned on the tap and began to wash her hands. Gold goop mixed with water, forming a glittering whirlpool as it ran down the drain.

But the hot, itchy sensation did not go away.

Alex scrubbed harder, hoping that the tingling feeling settling deep into her muscles was only her imagination. *Nothing terrible is wrong with me. This is just a delayed reaction to almost being run over by a truck and sprayed with icky gold stuff.*

A loud whirring noise began behind her, then stopped abruptly. Alex glanced over her shoulder. Nothing moved and no one else was in the garage. *Am I hearing things, too?* Alex wondered. She was dangerously close to panicking.

The itching suddenly got worse. Alex reached for the soap.

The shrill buzz of an electric saw rose above the sound of running water. Alex slowly turned her head to look at the tools on the wall. The electric saw had mysteriously switched on.

Confused and scared, Alex stared at it, wishing it would stop.

The saw instantly turned off.

Alex swallowed hard as she studied the saw. It wasn't plugged in. *How did it go on?*

She stepped away from the sink. As she walked past the large table holding the electric train set, power instantly surged through the wiring. The HO-gauge engine and cars started rolling around the figure eight layout.

What's happening? Alex watched as the train chugged up an incline past Annie's plastic dinosaurs. The engine bumped a purple-and-green *Tyrannosaurus rex* that was standing too close to the tracks and it fell off the table. Instinctively, Alex reached out to catch it.

Gold sparks shot from her fingers. Drawn to the current running through the system, the bolts struck the brass rails. The engine jumped off the track.

Jerking her hand back with a startled yelp, Alex held her breath. *Not possible,* she thought. Her eyes were playing tricks on her. Fingers could not generate electric sparks. Or could they? Exhaling slowly, Alex looked at her hands.

They started to glow.

No way!

Spinning on the heels of her soggy Doc Martens, Alex quickly stepped to the mirror hanging above the washer. The glow spread up her neck until her whole face shone with a golden light.

She screamed.

Raymond struggled through another scale on his saxophone, spun in a complete circle on the sidewalk, then pulled a potato chip from the open bag tucked into the bell of the horn. He looked up as he popped the chip into his mouth and stopped short.

The street was in chaos. A Paradise Valley Chemical truck was parked at an odd angle on the far side of the road, and the whole area was blocked off with yellow tape marked CAUTION. Water gushed from the fire hydrant the truck appeared to have hit.

Raymond blinked and tossed another chip into his mouth. *Something radical going down here*, he thought as he crunched and watched with curiosity.

Men in toxic waste suits swarmed around the back of the truck, which was covered with thick plastic sheets. Equipped with high-tech gear, the men were trying to contain and clean up something hidden behind the plastic shielding. Other men in dark business suits hovered a discreet distance from the accident taking notes, and a helicopter flew in a tight, circular pattern overhead.

Intrigued, Raymond hung around for a few minutes. It wasn't hard to figure out that some kind of dangerous chemical had spilled and contaminated the street. Covered from head to toe in protective gear, the clean-up crew wasn't taking any chances. They didn't want to be exposed.

With that realization, Raymond decided he had seen enough. Hanging around might be hazardous to *his* health. He decided to take the long way to Alex's house, staying as far from the accident as he could.

Alex was concentrating so hard on getting the awful, glowing stuff off her skin that she didn't hear Annie come in.

"Alex?" Annie walked slowly behind her, then dropped her book bag. "Tough first day, huh? What'd you do—go swimming in the sewer?"

Sighing heavily, Alex turned. Annie was staring at her, but not with the look of disgust she expected. A frown of questioning concern and astonishment creased her sister's brow.

"Annie . . ." Desperate, Alex blurted out an explanation. "I was coming home from school when this plant truck almost hit me and crashed right into a hydrant! Then a barrel of gold stuff spilled out all over me!"

Annie stared, her mouth open in disbelief. Taking a moment to recover her wits, she looked Alex in the eye. "Run that by me again. Slowly, this time."

Relieved that her sister hadn't run screaming from the garage, Alex told her the whole story again in more detail. ". . . and just by looking at them, I think I turned on the saw and the electric train set!"

Annie studied Alex with thoughtful curiosity. "You're not clever enough to make this up. Did you tell Mom?"

Alex shook her head. "Not yet." She looked up with pleading eyes. Her sister was a genius. If anyone could figure out what was going on, Annie could. "I feel really weird. Should I go to the doctor?"

"Maybe." Annie frowned. "Better let me check you out first." Wasting no time, she pulled a worn medical bag from a neat stack of scientific supplies and equipment.

Alex let Annie draw her away from the sink, and she tried not to flinch under the older girl's scrutiny. "It's gonna be all right, Alex. Okay?" Annie said.

Alex nodded. She wasn't sure she believed her sister, but there was genuine worry in Annie's tone. For a moment, she felt better. But then Annie's eyes widened with enthusiastic delight.

"Whoa! You're glowing like a neon sign!"

My sister, the mad scientist, Alex thought despondently as she sat on an overturned milk crate. *And I'm the experiment of the day.*

Vince stood in the street, supervising the cleanup operation at the accident site. He imagined Danielle Atron pacing in her office and talking into the speakerphone on her desk as he gave his report as calmly as he could. The toxic waste crews were efficient, and all traces of the spilled GC 161 would soon be gone.

"Driver said some kid stepped into the road and he had to swerve to avoid him."

As always, the CEO remained unflustered, but Vince heard the tension in her crisp voice.

"Him?" Danielle asked coldly.

"Or her," Vince said evenly. "He says he didn't get a good look. I've kept the police away from here so far."

"This is an absolute disaster." The CEO's voice rose slightly, a sure sign that she was very angry.

Vince braced himself for a more alarmed reaction to his final, not-so-good bit of news. "There's one more detail you're not going to like." He said in an unruffled tone that masked his own anger at Dave. "He says that when the

GC One-Sixty-One spilled out of the truck, it drenched the kid.''

''What?'' Danielle almost, but not quite, yelled.

''I'm afraid so.'' Turning toward the vacant lot, Vince scowled at the driver who was responsible for the accident. Dave was kneeling by a small depression in the lot. ''But we found a handprint in the mud near the accident, and I'm hoping we can match the kid with it.''

''Vince.'' Danielle strained to stay calm now. ''I know nothing about GC One-Sixty-One. I know nothing about an accident, and I know nothing about this kid until you find and bring him to me.''

''I'll take care of it,'' Vince assured her.

''Like you took care of this?'' Danielle snapped.

Vince flinched and pocketed his phone as Danielle clicked off. His hard, blue gaze swept across the vacant lot and surrounding houses. For the first time since coming to work at Paradise Valley Chemical, he had made a mistake in judgment and had let his boss down.

He had been in charge of the critical transport of the secret compound, and the delivery had been botched. He had allowed Dave to drive, knowing the man was incompetent, and he felt personally responsible for the accident.

And some unidentified kid had been exposed to GC 161 and was running around loose.

The plant had developed and transported the experimental compound illegally. Danielle Atron's career was at stake.

So was his.

Vince vowed to find the missing kid and deliver him or her to the CEO—one way or another.

CHAPTER 5

Annie's methodical approach to the problem had a soothing effect on Alex. As the gold stuff dried, the itching began to stop. Alex didn't know if that was good or not, but not feeling itchy made it easier to sit still while Annie checked her vital signs.

Alex sighed as Annie wrote the results in a loose-leaf notebook. Annie had never paid much attention to her in the past, except to tease her or boss her around. Becoming her sister's priority-one science project wasn't exactly the same as finding out that Annie actually *liked* her, but it was better than being ignored.

And Alex needed her. Annie was smart, and Alex was scared. She jumped as Annie unfastened the Velcro cuff of the blood pressure device, removed it, and set it aside.

"Your blood pressure and body temperature are normal. How do you feel?"

"I don't know." Alex could see the halo of the pulsing light reflected in the mirror. Her face was still glowing, but at least the glowing didn't hurt or itch. "My legs and arms are all tingly. What do you think it is?"

"I don't know. Might be nothing."

"So, I shouldn't worry?" Alex asked hopefully.

"Of course you should worry!" Annie paused, then began speaking in a low, sinister voice, her brown eyes glinting with macabre joy. "For all we know, you could have been hit by something that's seeping into your brain cells at this very minute, about to attack your central nervous system and turn you into a quivering mass of jelly."

"Annie!" Alex shivered. She knew Annie was kidding, but what if she was right?

The side door of the garage opened and Raymond bounced in, closing the door behind him. He turned, looked at Alex, and gasped. "Whoa! What happened to you?"

Alex sagged, too depressed to reply.

"Alex was involved in a little . . . accident." Annie smiled awkwardly.

"An accident?" Raymond stared at Alex. "You mean the one near school?"

"You know about that?" Alex asked with surprise.

"I just came from there!" Raymond said excitedly. "The place is going nuts!"

Panic threatened to overwhelm Alex again, and she looked at Annie in desperation.

"Listen," Annie insisted. "All of us have to relax, okay? So Alex is glowing a little. No big deal."

"No big deal?" Raymond stared at Annie in amazement. "No big deal? Look at her!"

Alex met Annie's direct gaze, then glanced at Raymond's troubled face. She was still glowing.

How were they going to explain *that* to her parents? Or the school?

Life as she knew it was over.

Tabloid headlines flashed through Alex's mind: Alex Mack, the Human Light Bulb.

With a look of grim determination, Annie pulled her microscope from under the train table. "We need more data."

Alex looked into Annie's dark brown eyes. Her sister *was* worried about her. Really worried.

Raymond crossed to the opposite side of the garage, dropped his things on the floor, and sat on a high stool to watch.

Alex didn't blame him for keeping his distance. Maybe all it took to turn someone into a neon lamp was a tiny bit of the gold stuff. Annie, however, was too intent on studying the shining gunk to worry about that possibility. She carefully scraped a little of the stuff from Alex's skin onto a glass slide and placed it under the microscope.

Leaning forward in unison, Alex and Raymond stared at Annie as she peered through the eyepiece. Long moments passed before she volunteered an opinion.

"I get the feeling this wasn't some minor accident. I've never seen anything like this stuff before." Annie motioned for Alex to take a look.

Alex gazed through the microscope at the magnified sample of the fluid. Globules of lighter gold swam in a glowing, golden ooze. She sat back down with a shudder.

"Besides," Annie continued, "if all those security guys were out there, this has got to be something big."

"They'll blame *you*." Raymond threw his hands up in the air. "Adults always do."

"It wasn't my fault," Alex insisted.

Annie shook her head. "He's right. We'd better not tell anyone until this dies down."

"Not even Mom and Dad?" Alex asked.

"No one!" Annie said sharply. "*Especially* Mom and Dad. They'd want to rush you off to the hospital."

"That might not be a bad idea." Raymond eyed Annie narrowly. "We don't know what this gold stuff has done to Alex. What if it's eating away at her—''

Annie cut him off. ''All her vital signs are normal. And I know that any substance the chemical plant developed that can make someone glow has to be experimental. For Alex's sake, we can't tell anyone. At least, not yet.''

Raymond scowled, then nodded. ''Okay.''

Alex barely heard them. Her stomach growled, and all she could think about was food. ''Wow, I'm really hungry all of a sudden. Ray, can I have some chips?''

''How can you think about eating at a time like this?'' Ray asked incredulously.

''Because I'm really hungry.'' Alex stared at the open bag of chips lying on the workbench behind him. Her stomach growled louder, demanding food. She *had* to have something to eat, and there wasn't anything in the garage except Ray's chips. Her thoughts focused on the plastic bag.

The bag suddenly flew off the bench. Suspended in midair, it moved across the garage on a direct course toward Alex.

Annie's gaze fastened on the airborne bag of

chips as it slowed and hovered before Alex. Alex grabbed it.

"Did Alex do that?" Raymond stared in disbelief.

Astonished, Annie shrugged. "Apparently."

"Cool!" Raymond grinned.

Enormously pleased with herself, Alex popped a chip into her mouth and chewed contentedly. Maybe some of the side effects of the strange, gold liquid wouldn't be so bad after all.

Vince pressed the button on the slide projector's remote control, and the picture of another Paradise Valley teenager appeared on the screen. "Annette Wayne." He glanced at Dave, who was sitting beside him.

Dave shook his head.

Another click on the button and another picture.

"Neil Consella."

Dave just shook his head and fanned himself with his hat.

"Come on, pal. Give me something." Vince was running out of patience. "You're the only one who was there."

And that's the unfortunate truth, Vince thought angrily. Dave *was* the only person who could identify the kid that had been doused with the compound.

"I told you, Vince. I didn't get a good look. It all happened so fast."

Triggering another photo, Vince glanced at the name on his master list. Alexandra Mack. He didn't bother saying the name aloud. Dave just stared at the smiling image of the long-haired girl on the screen, his face a complete blank. Annoyed, Vince stood up and moved in front of Dave, blocking his view.

Dave just blinked.

"Well," Vince said evenly, hoping to prompt a reaction from the dim-witted driver. "We know the kid was either from the junior high or high school and was headed home on foot."

Dave nodded.

"The boys in the lab promise to have the handprint ID unit finished by tomorrow. You"— Vince leaned forward and poked Dave in the chest to make sure the driver was listening—

"you will report to me in the morning. As soon as I have that device, we'll go door-to-door until we find that kid. Understand?"

"No, but I'll be here." Dave frowned in puzzlement. "What's a handprint ID unit?"

Vince didn't try to explain. He just laughed softly to himself. He was looking forward to the hunt. It satisfied his predatory instincts. Armed with the identification device that could electronically match the handprint taken from the mud with the actual hand of the GC 161 victim, he did not doubt that he would succeed. "I'll find this kid."

"Can we grab a bite to eat before we start?" Dave asked.

Vince sighed wearily. Dave was a moron. He was also the only witness, so Vince was stuck with him until the job was done.

"You're not glowing anymore," Annie said casually, hiding her intense excitement.

Annie couldn't get over the fact that her younger sister had accidently been transformed into someone so interesting. Visions of fame and respect from the world's scientific community—

and all before she reached eighteen and had graduated from high school—flashed through her mind. Alex's intriguing condition was just too good to be true.

Alex bubbled with relief. "Maybe it was just a temporary thing—huh, Annie?"

"Yeah, maybe." Scowling as that possibility became evident and her dreams of scientific achievement evaporated. Annie nodded and took a swig of water from a bottle. Lost in thought, she ignored the gurgling sound beside her. *Bye-bye Nobel Prize.* She heaved a sigh and stared wistfully into space.

"Hey, Annie . . ."

Raymond's voice pierced Annie's reverie, and she turned. He was standing by the sink looking seriously concerned.

"Where did Alex go?"

But Alex herself had no idea.

One moment she was herself. The next she felt a tingling sensation throughout her entire body . . . and suddenly she was on the floor.

How did I fall? she wondered. *And what's wrong with me? I feel all oozy and weird. . . .* "Annie?" she tried to say. But her voice came out funny. "Annie? What's happening?"

Replacing the cap on the bottle, Annie glanced around the garage. No Alex. Puzzled, she looked down and felt her heart skip a beat. Alex's clothes and shoes were lying on the floor, and a puddle of clear ooze was slowly emerging from the pile.

She distinctly heard the puddle make a gurgling sound.

"I . . . I think that's her!" Annie gasped, her gaze never leaving the puddle that looked like watered-down, colorless Jell-O.

"Yeah, right." Raymond laughed nervously. "Stop it, Annie. Really." His amusement changed to fear as the puddle suddenly picked up speed and headed straight for him.

Annie didn't know whether to be thrilled because scientific fame and fortune were still within her grasp or horrified because her sister really had turned into a quivering mass of jelly.

"Annie!" Raymond moved closer to the older girl. "Do something!"

"Alex!" Annie shouted, not knowing what else to do. "Stop fooling around!"

Raymond climbed a metal shelving unit and hung on. The puddle stopped, but Annie's relief was short-lived.

A loud knock sounded on the side door and a voice called out. "Kids! Are you in there?"

Dad!

CHAPTER 6

Alex was terrified.

She had no idea how she had suddenly turned into a pile of clear gelatinous stuff. One minute she had been a girl, then a hot tingling sensation had surged through her body and she was a puddle. Worse, she didn't know if she could change back into herself again. Being a liquid wasn't exactly unpleasant, but she didn't want to spend the rest of her life as a glob of ooze.

She hadn't meant to scare Raymond, either. The unexpected transformation had confused her, and she had run to him for help. Raymond was her best friend, after all. *Or my ex-best friend*, Alex thought sadly. *Who wants to pal around with a blob of jelly?*

The sound of her father's voice at the door made her jiggle with fright. Although she no longer had eyes or ears, she could see and hear everything.

"Alex, hide!" Annie hissed. "Get under the table." Then she wheeled on Raymond. "Ray, don't say a word."

"Right." Ray kept a wary eye on Alex.

Gurgling, Alex glided under the table and positioned herself so she could watch and listen.

Annie raced to the door to intercept their father, but Mr. Mack pushed it open just before she reached it.

"Hey, Dad. What's up?" Annie smiled brightly, then turned toward the workbench, pretending to be in the middle of a project.

"Boy, am I glad to see you, Annie." Mr. Mack glanced at Ray and smiled. "Hey, Ray."

Still stunned, Ray managed a weak smile.

Stuffing his hands in his trouser pockets, Mr.

Mack leaned toward Annie. "Have you kids seen Alex?"

"Alex?" Annie didn't look up. "Nope. She apparently stayed late at school to try out . . . for the basketball team. Right, Ray?"

"Right," Raymond said with an exaggerated nod.

Annie fiddled with the wiring on the train set. "Basketball?" Mr. Mack said uncertainly. "I didn't know she liked basketball."

"Neither did I. She's been just full of surprises lately." Annie was so nervous, she flinched slightly when her father patted her shoulder affectionately.

"Well, as long as we know where she is." Noticing the derailed train, Mr. Mack moved toward the table to set the engine and cars back on the tracks.

Alex didn't react quickly enough, and squealed when he stepped on the edge of her puddle-self. "Ouch!" Her voice wavered like she was talking underwater.

"What was that?" Mr. Mack stooped down to peer under the table.

Alex quickly slithered over a hammer and between two cardboard boxes full of Annie's scientific equipment. The warm tingling through her began to get hotter.

"It was me," Annie said. "I, uh—stuck my finger on a wire."

Desperately hoping Annie could keep their dad distracted, Alex slid toward the back edge of the table.

"Are you all right?" Standing up, Mr. Mack looked at Annie with mild concern.

"Fine!"

Nodding, Mr. Mack headed for the door that led from the garage to the kitchen.

Alex gathered herself, then shot across the floor to a stack of boxes against the back wall. However, she misjudged her speed and slammed into a metal garbage can. The rattling crash rang through the garage. *Uh-oh* . . .

Raymond instantly stumbled backward into the metal shelves, almost knocking them over, hoping to cover for Alex's noise.

Mr. Mack looked back with a questioning frown.

"Watch it, Ray!" Annie snapped, then turned away from her father to wink at Raymond. The shaking shelves didn't sound exactly like the trash can, but even she had to admire Ray's quick thinking.

"Sorry," Raymond said, grabbing the metal shelving unit to steady it. "Lost my balance."

"Uh-huh." Perplexed, Mr. Mack glanced at Annie. "What's Raymond doing here without Alex?"

"Uh—he's helping me with a new science project."

Mr. Mack eyed her suspiciously. It wasn't a secret that Annie thought Raymond was a bit of a flake and a pest.

Annie quickly explained. "I'm going to adjust his molecular structure and try to change him into a human puddle."

Not funny, Annie, Alex thought as she flattened herself against the floor. *What if I'm doomed to be a puddle forever?*

Mr. Mack looked at Raymond again, then realized that Annie was joking and chuckled. "As long as you clean up the mess afterward," he cautioned with mock sternness.

Annie waved over her shoulder as Mr. Mack left. She waited a moment, then began an anxious search of the garage. "Okay, Alex. You can come out now."

Relief surged through Alex, and her liquid structure slowly assumed human size and shape. Then suddenly, she was herself.

Or almost. Annie and Raymond stared at Alex, speechless.

Alex was stark naked. Fortunately, she had materialized behind the boxes and only her head and shoulders were visible. *Still. . . .* Gasping with embarrassment, she looked pleadingly at Annie. "Bring me my clothes."

Giggling, Annie gathered up Alex's soggy clothing and handed them to Alex. "Turn around, Raymond."

Raymond hesitated for a split second.

Alex's eyes narrowed, and suddenly Raymond spun around so he was facing the sink.

"What the—" Raymond squealed with surprised indignation. "How'd you . . . Okay, okay! I was just going to—"

"Did you do that?" Annie asked.

Nodding, Alex laughed. "Yeah. I just thought about turning Raymond around, and—presto—he turned around. It was easy."

Annie wasn't amused. She studied Alex with a serious frown. "How did you turn into a liquid?"

Alex shrugged as she struggled into her wet T-shirt. "I was watching you drink water, and the next thing I knew, I was slithering around on the floor!"

"You metamorphosed."

"Huh?" Alex blinked.

"Changed from one state to another," Annie said impatiently. "Transformed from a solid into a liquid and back again. You can . . . *morph* is a good word for it. Fewer syllables."

"Can I turn around now?" Raymond asked.

In a flash Raymond was spinning around and around on the balls of his feet.

"Alex?" Annie touched Alex's arm.

Alex stared at Raymond as he whirled around, fascinated and scared. She had just thought about turning him back around, not transforming him into a human top with no off-switch. She didn't know what to do!

"Alex!" Holding her by the shoulders, Annie forced Alex to look at her. "Concentrate! Concentrate on making Raymond stand still. Think *stop*."

Alex focused on Raymond. *Stop spinning, stop spinning . . .*

Raymond stopped spinning—abruptly. Dizzy, he staggered and grabbed on to the sink to keep from falling down.

Radical, Alex thought. She couldn't believe she had done all that with her thoughts. "Fantastic!" she said aloud.

Raymond did not share her enthusiasm. He glared at her as he stumbled toward the outside door. "Thanks a lot, Alex. I thought I was your friend."

"Ray, I'm sorry. I couldn't help it!"

Pausing at the door, Raymond glared at Alex. "Well, you're going to have to learn. When you figure out how to control these weird things you can do, let me know." He left.

"Ray . . ." Upset, Alex slumped against the dryer. It immediately turned on. She jumped away from the machine with a startled glance at Annie. "What?"

"Ray's right, Alex. You've got to learn to control these powers, or you'll be in more trouble than you can imagine."

"I *can* control them," Alex insisted stubbornly. She turned off the dryer with a quick glance. "See?"

Both girls turned as the kitchen door opened.

"Alex! When did you get home?" Mrs. Mack walked in and crossed to the far wall.

"A few minutes ago," Alex said.

"Your father's been looking for you." Turning her back to the girls, Mrs. Mack scanned the tool rack. "Have either of you seen the hammer?"

Annie shook her head. "No, I haven't."

Alex knew exactly where the hammer was. She had seen it when she was under the train table. Her gaze and her mind both focused on the handle of the missing tool before she could stop herself. The hammer slid out from under the table, across the floor, and into her hand.

"Here it is," Alex said, avoiding Annie's narrowed gaze.

Mrs. Mack turned with a smile. "Oh, thanks, honey." Taking the hammer, she started back into the house. "Your turn to set the table, Alex."

"Coming."

"What's next, Alex?" Annie asked with a wry laugh. "Flying dishes around the kitchen?"

"Just chill, Annie. Okay?" Alex hurried after her mother. She wasn't about to let anything spoil the thrill of her new powers.

Danielle Atron was furious.

Vince stood stiffly before the CEO in her office as she told him in no uncertain terms what she thought about his security measures.

"There's no excuse for such incompetence, Vince." Danielle rose, leaned across the top of her polished desk, and glared menacingly at him. "This situation must be salvaged."

"I understand, Ms. Atron."

"Do you?" Straightening, Danielle crossed her arms over her chest. "I assume you have a plan."

"Yes. After I get the handprint ID unit tomorrow, Dave and I will begin the search. We'll check every house, every street and alley until that kid is found."

"Dave?" Danielle raised an eyebrow. "Isn't he the driver who crashed the truck and dumped GC One-Sixty-One on the kid in the first place?"

"Yes, but—"

"You should have fired him immediately."

"Nothing would please me more, Ms. Atron," Vince said. "Unfortunately, he's the only witness. He saw the kid and might be able to identify him . . . or her."

"I see." Danielle turned her back on him and strolled to the window. "You will investigate every youngster that even remotely resembles the one Dave saw. Do I make myself clear?"

"Perfectly."

"Have a good night's sleep, kid, wherever you are," Danielle said as she gazed out over her domain. "You won't have many more."

Vince was very glad he wasn't the kid.

CHAPTER 7

Alex was up and dressed before Annie the next morning. They had hardly had a chance to speak since dinner the night before. *Just as well*, Alex thought. When she had tried to take a bath before going to bed, she couldn't stop herself from liquifying. Luckily, her gloppy self didn't mix with water. Annie could probably explain that, too, but Alex didn't want to admit she was having trouble.

Alex studied herself in the dresser mirror. She was wearing overalls and a long-sleeved, black-

and-red striped T-shirt. She flipped a blue cap backward on her head. She still looked like the old Alex Mack. But today, everything would be different, she decided. She had a second chance at a fresh start, and she was determined not to foul it up.

Glancing at the disarray on her side of the room, Alex decided that now might be a good time to get organized. She lifted a book off the floor with her thoughts and steered it toward the bookcase.

"Alex!" Annie said sharply from behind her.

Alex lost control of the book. It whipped sideways as though propelled from a slingshot and slammed into a framed picture on the wall, breaking the glass.

"Don't do that, Annie! You startled me." Alex stared at the shattered picture. She'd have to clean up the broken glass before leaving for school. Her mother had long ago given up trying to get her to clean her half of the room on a regular basis, but Mrs. Mack wouldn't tolerate this.

Annie glared at Alex. "*I* didn't do anything.

You can't keep fooling around with these powers of yours until we know more about them."

"Why not? They're not dangerous or anything."

"Not dangerous?" Annie advanced until she was looking Alex in the eye from a distance of three inches. "You can turn yourself into a liquid, shoot bolts of electricity from the tips of your fingers, and you're telekinetic. The potential for disaster seems obvious to me."

Alex frowned. "Tele—what?"

"Telekinetic." Picking up the book, Annie shook it in Alex's face. "You can move things with your mind." She poked Alex in the head with her finger. "Duh."

"Oh." Alex hated it when Annie made fun of her. Really hated it. She wasn't stupid. She just wasn't a genius, like her sister.

"And you're totally out of control, Alex." After shoving the book in the bookcase, Annie paused with her hand on her chin. "I've been thinking about all this since yesterday afternoon. The problem is one of concentration."

Annie began to pace, talking to the floor rather

than to her sister. It was a habit that had always angered Alex, but now she paid attention.

"When you concentrate on having something, it comes to you. If you think about water, you turn into a puddle. A good first step would be to learn how to distract yourself when you're in danger of losing control."

"Distract myself?" Alex asked.

"Yeah. Recite something in your head. Anything that's boring but requires intense thought. For you it could be something fairly simple—like the multiplication tables or even nursery rhymes."

"I don't have to stand here and be insulted, Annie."

Annie's expression softened. "I'm just worried about you, okay? I want to help, but you've got to listen to me and take my advice, or you'll have more trouble than you can handle. I mean it."

"Well, maybe you worry too much, Annie!" Eyes flashing, Alex stomped out of the room, then abruptly turned back. "I'm not one of your science projects."

"Alex . . ."

Ignoring her, Alex bounded down the stairs and into the kitchen. Suddenly, she was very hungry.

As usual, her father was working on the portable computer at the kitchen table. Her mother was on the phone and making toast at the same time.

". . . not according to our demographics." Mrs. Mack dropped two pieces of bread into the toaster, then walked away without pushing the lever down. "That approach won't influence anyone between eighteen and twenty-five, and that's your target market."

Without thinking, Alex looked at the toaster. Her stomach growled. The lever slid down and engaged. With a slight gasp, she glanced at her parents. Neither was paying attention. Sagging with relief, Alex pulled out a chair and sat down.

"Morning, Dad."

"Alex," Mr. Mack said absently. He waved away a fly buzzing around his head, but his attention remained on the screen.

Annie came in and threw her book bag on the floor next to the back door. Sliding into the chair

73

at the far side of the table, she fixed Alex with a glowering stare.

Alex looked away as her mother handed her a plate of warm, freshly buttered toast.

"Why aren't you wearing your new boots, Alex?" Mrs. Mack asked with a glance at Alex's feet.

"Yes, Alex," Annie said, sneering sweetly. "Why aren't you wearing your new boots?"

"Uh, because—" *Think fast, Alex!* "Uh, they're not broken in yet—and they hurt my feet."

"Then maybe we should take them back and get a pair that fits properly," Mrs. Mack suggested.

"That's a good idea." Raising an eyebrow, Annie silently challenged Alex to talk her way out of this situation.

Alex scowled at her smug sister. Alex knew she'd have to earn the money to replace the ruined Doc Martens.

"That's not necessary, Mom." Alex smiled sweetly. "If I wear them every other day, they'll be fine in a week or so."

"Okay," Mrs. Mack said absently, as if she had already turned her attention elsewhere. She dialed another number and poured herself a cup of coffee. "Mr. Walker, please. Mrs. Mack calling." She wandered into the living room with the portable phone to her ear, carrying her coffee.

"What's wrong, Dad?" Annie asked. "You look a little worried this morning."

The fly landed on Alex's arm. She shook it off.

Mr. Mack frowned and shook his head. "There must be something wrong with the remote access systems at the plant. I can't open the GC One-Sixty-One file."

A thoughtful look clouded Annie's face.

The fly landed on Alex's toast. Irritated, Alex raised her hand to shoo it away. A green bolt of energy shot from her finger and into the unfortunate fly. Her golden brown toast blackened into inedible char.

Mr. Mack was so intent on the access problem that he hadn't seen anything.

Furious, Annie glared at Alex.

"Hey!" Raymond shouted at the back door. "Let me in. The door's locked!" He banged insistently.

Alex glanced toward the door and smiled. Maybe Raymond wasn't mad at her anymore! The dead bolt turned.

"*Alex!*" Annie hissed.

"Gotta go!" Jumping out of her chair, Alex grabbed her bag and dumped the burned toast into the garbage disposal. Turning on the water, she flicked the disposal switch and felt her arms get hot and tingly. She immediately turned off the tap.

Basketball. Homework. She tried to think of anything but water. The tingling persisted. *Scott . . . Scott . . .* Even thinking about Scott couldn't stop the transformation so she concentrated on keeping her clothes and backpack with her, this time.

As Alex melted into a puddle on the kitchen floor, she saw Annie's horrified gaze.

Mr. Mack's eyes were focused on the computer.

Raymond pounded on the door.

Mrs. Mack stuck her head through the living room doorway. "Let him in before he breaks down the door, Annie," she ordered. "Where's Alex?"

"Uh, she had to get something from the garage."

Mr. Mack remained unaware of the unfolding drama.

Mrs. Mack put her coffee cup in the sink, then noticed the large puddle on the floor. "Clean that up, will you, Annie? I'm late. And remind me to call a plumber. There must be a leak under the sink." With that, she swept out of the kitchen.

As Annie rose and opened the back door, the puddle that was Alex followed. It slithered through the opening, zipped around Raymond's white high-tops and into the shrubbery.

Upset and unable to re-form, Alex kept going along the foundation of the house. Thorns and sharp branches scratched and poked her jelly sides, and they hurt. Clearly her puddle-self was not immune to pain.

Alex materialized a few minutes later on the far side of the garage. Raymond and Annie were scouring the bushes, calling her name. Angry at herself for losing control, she didn't need the additional hassle of Annie reminding her that she had been warned.

Thirteen and nearly grown-up, Alex was tired of living with her older sister's brilliance and her superior attitude about everything, especially Alex's new wondrous powers. They were *her* powers, Alex thought stubbornly, and she would learn to control them without Annie's help.

Cutting through the neighbor's yard, Alex waited on the next block for Raymond to catch up.

Sitting in a black humvee, Vince glanced at the rectangular metal box stashed between the front seats. The guys in the lab had worked all night to finish the handprint ID units. A second, backup unit was stowed behind the driver's seat.

Impatient to begin surveillance of Danielle Atron Junior High, Vince checked his watch, then glanced in the rearview mirror. Dave was running across the parking lot with a large, paper grocery sack. He was five minutes late.

"Sorry, Vince." Huffing and puffing, he slid into the passenger seat and pushed the brim of his cap off his forehead.

Sorry, Vince. How many times would he hear those two words again today? Vince wondered as he gunned the engine and raced off the plant property. He didn't acknowledge Dave for a couple of minutes. He was sorry he had ever laid eyes on the bumbling driver. However, when Dave reached into the bag and pulled out a box of powdered doughnuts, he didn't have a choice. He had to say something.

"What do you think you're doing?"

Dave's face blanked as he considered the question. "Having breakfast?" White sugar fell like snow onto his dark blue trousers as he took a bite, then offered the box to Vince. "Want a doughnut?"

"No! And there's no eating in company cars!" Vince snapped. "Look at the mess you're making."

Dave glanced at the white spots on his lap, then brushed the sugar onto the floor and seat. "Sorry, Vince."

"Sorry, Vince," Vince muttered under his breath, then ran a hand over his short hair. "Put those away," he demanded.

"I gotta eat, Vince." Dave swallowed hard. "I

can't concentrate if I'm hungry. We gotta find that kid, right?"

"Yeah, right." Vince surrendered without further argument. As long as he identified the kid, Danielle Atron would be happy and his damaged reputation would be saved. Someone else could worry about cleaning up Dave's trash.

Setting the box of doughnuts on top of the ID unit, Dave grinned and dusted sugar off his hands. Then, he helped himself to another one.

But, Vince thought with a weary sigh, *it's going to be a very long day.*

The lawn around the courtyard near the front doors of the school was filled with groups of kids hanging out before the first bell rang.

Alex slowed as she drew near, her high spirits plummeting. Anxious to see if he had made it into the band, Raymond had already gone into the building to check the posted list. Without him or Nicole and Robyn, Alex felt completely alone. Scanning the crowd for others she might know, she strolled down the walk around the edge of the lawn.

"Outta the way!" A voice rang out behind her.

Alex glanced over her shoulder, then jumped onto the grass to avoid being run down by a boy on a speeding bicycle. She thudded into someone, jumped back, then groaned when she realized whom she had hit—Jessica. The older girl's notebook flipped open when it hit the ground, and the papers tucked into the cover pocket spilled out.

"You again!" Jessica's friends turned to stare at Alex. The fallen ninth grader got to her feet as gracefully as possible and took a menacing step forward, the notebook forgotten in her anger. "You're not even an accident *waiting* to happen, are you? You just happen! To me!"

"I'm really sorry," Alex said with genuine regret. "That boy on the bike—"

"I don't want to know, okay? Just stay away from me!"

"What's the problem now?" Scott asked as he trotted toward the gathering crowd. He glanced with curiosity at Alex, but focused his attention on Jessica.

"Problem? This little seventh-grade—*troll*,

that's the problem." Rubbing her arm, Jessica continued to glare at Alex.

Scott frowned at Jessica, then turned to Alex.

"Jessica!" The tall girl Alex recognized as Ellen from the basketball court the day before shrieked as a sudden gust of wind swept across the lawn, scattering Jessica's papers. Jessica and her friends scrambled to retrieve them. Scott hesitated, looked at Alex, then ran to help.

Mortified, Alex dashed toward the front doors, into the school, and directly across the path of Vice Principal Heller.

"Halt!" the stocky man commanded loudly.

Alex skidded to a stop and waited breathlessly as the vice principal scowled at her.

"Mack, isn't it?" he asked sternly.

Alex nodded, aware that several other students had paused to watch the spectacle.

"There's no running in the halls, Ms. Mack. Do you understand?"

Alex nodded again, too embarrassed to answer aloud.

"Well, do you?" Heller asked, his frown deepening as he leaned closer to stare at her face.

"Are you sick, Ms. Mack? Your color seems a bit off—"

Alex looked at her hands. With a gasp of alarm, she bolted for the girls' room.

"Walk!" Mr. Heller's voice boomed through the hall.

Alex ran.

She was starting to glow.

CHAPTER 8

Two girls glanced at Alex as she burst through the door.

Holding her bag up to hide her glowing face, Alex rushed into a stall, slammed the door, and locked it. She perched on the edge of the toilet and drew her legs back, then positioned her backpack under the door as additional shielding. Her knees and shins were shining with the golden light, too.

Whispering and giggling, the girls left.

Then the first period bell rang.

Still glowing like a floodlight, Alex knew she couldn't leave. She had never felt more miserable in her life. She was late for math class for the second day in a row, she'd made an enemy of the most popular girl in school, and the boy of her dreams thought she was worse than hopelessly ordinary. *I'm a total jerk*, she thought. Things could not possibly be worse.

A toilet two stalls down flushed.

Uh-oh!

The sound of water rushing through pipes suddenly dominated her thoughts, and Alex couldn't stop the transformation process.

Panicked, she threw her legs forward to stand up and accidentally kicked her backpack out toward the sinks. In an instant, she changed from being a depressed teenaged girl into a mass of clear jelly. Oozing onto the floor, she slid over to the corner of the stall.

A pair of white sneakers attached to tan legs paused outside the stall. Alex stretched herself along the seam between the back wall and the floor. She'd be in even more trouble if the girl called maintenance to clean up a mess before she could become herself again.

"Anybody here?" The girl called out as she bent over and peered under the door.

Alex stiffened, but the girl didn't see anything unusual and stood up again. She picked up Alex's backpack and took it with her when she left.

Alone again, Alex flowed under the stall door. A minute later, she materialized. She was now seven minutes late for math, but she had to find her backpack first. The girl had probably taken it to the Lost-and-Found, which, Alex realized with a defeated sigh, was in the school office.

Footsteps echoing in the deserted corridor, Alex hurried toward the office and met Mr. Heller coming out the glass door.

"Feeling better, Ms. Mack?" He did not seem angry, but concerned.

"Yes," Alex said with relief. "Something I ate for breakfast must have disagreed with me."

Mr. Heller nodded. "You're late for class."

"Uh, I—" Alex swallowed hard and tried not to shake.

"The receptionist will give you a pass."

"Thank you," Alex whispered as she moved to enter the office.

"Don't let me catch you running in the halls again."

"No, sir. You won't."

Never again, Alex thought as she identified her bag and waited for the receptionist to fill out her pink hall pass. From now on she intended to keep a low profile and steer clear of anything and anyone that might trigger the effects of her strange, new condition at inconvenient times.

That wouldn't be hard. She was already an invisible face in the crowd. Nobody except Raymond, Robyn, and Nicole knew or cared about plain, old, ordinary Alex Mack.

Vince parked the humvee across the street from the junior high school.

"How long do we have to wait here?" Dave fidgeted with the sealed plastic wrapping on a bag of pretzels.

"Until the last class is dismissed." Vince's hands tightened on the steering wheel and he counted to ten. The sound of crackling plastic grated on his nerves. "All the kids in town are in school. Driving around would be a waste of time."

"Yeah," Dave agreed absently.

"But they eat lunch outside, and they all take P.E. If you recognize the kid before school lets out, it'll save everyone a lot of time and trouble."

"Uh-huh." Dave tried to tear the plastic with his teeth, then gripped the sides of the bag with both hands and yanked. The bag tore open and pretzels flew everywhere. "Sorry, Vince."

"Yeah." Vince picked a pretzel off his lap and tossed it out the window.

Somehow, Alex managed to get through the rest of the morning, lunch, and her first afternoon class without further incident. Stopping by her locker to get her English book, Alex fumbled in her backpack for the paper with the combination.

"Well, well. If it isn't the walking accident."

Jessica paused three lockers down, twirled her lock, and opened the door in a flash. Stashing one book and removing another, she turned slightly and looked Alex up and down. Ellen waited behind her.

"Thanks to you, I have to do an extra assignment because I lost my English homework." Jessica scowled.

"I'm really sorry. I didn't mean—"

"Of course, you didn't mean it. You can't help it if you're completely lacking in cool." Jessica laughed and shook her head. "I mean really. Who does your hair? The gardener?"

A red flush blossomed on Alex's cheeks. She lowered her eyes, wishing the day was over and that Jessica would go away. She didn't want any trouble. It just seemed to happen around her.

"Give it a rest, Jessica," said a sharp, determined voice.

Alex looked up as Robyn and Nicole paused between her and Jessica. Frowning with worry, Robyn hovered nearby as Nicole boldly challenged the older girl.

"What's it to you?" Jessica asked flippantly.

Nicole stepped forward, refusing to be intimidated.

Robyn placed a restraining hand on her arm and issued a nervous warning. "Nicole ... don't."

Nicole ignored her and fixed Jessica with a

fiery, direct gaze. "Alex isn't bothering you. Leave her alone."

"And who's gonna make me? You?"

"If I have to." Nicole's blazing eyes never wavered.

"Stop it, Nicole. We're gonna get us all into trouble."

"Robyn! Chill." Nicole set her jaw and jutted her chin, daring Jessica to try something.

Alex looked from one face to the other. Jessica's expression was one of disdain. Robyn looked like she was waiting for a bomb to fall. Nicole was angry but seemed to be enjoying herself.

"Get lost," Jessica said as she turned back to her locker. Ellen drifted away.

Robyn grabbed Nicole by the back of her shirt.

Alex suddenly realized that, like Scott, Nicole was rising to her defense and trying to rescue her. And she was just standing there doing nothing. *What am I anyway?* Alex asked herself angrily. *A spineless coward as well as a hopeless nerd.* She had to stand up for herself and fight her own battles. What little self-respect she had left demanded it.

Alex eased toward Jessica. A lump formed in her throat and her heart rate increased. She didn't know what she was going to say, but she had to do something.

As Alex got closer, she saw the neatly stacked books and carefully arranged personal items in Jessica's locker. A vision of the contents flying out of the locker and down the hallway filled her mind. Too fast for Alex to stop it, her telekinetic power engaged.

Jessica yelped and jumped back as everything in her locker spilled onto the floor at her feet.

Nicole and Robin gasped, then choked back startled laughter.

Vice Principal Heller yelled and came striding down the hallway toward them.

Stunned, Alex just stared at the mess. She had thought about dumping Jessica's things, but she hadn't meant to do it.

"Okay, girls," Mr. Heller barked. "That's enough!"

All four girls looked at him in openmouthed fright.

"You again, Ms. Mack." He zeroed in on Alex, then frowned at Nicole, Robyn, and Jessica. Dedicated to maintaining law and order in the halls of Danielle Atron Junior High, Mr. Heller would not listen to any explanations. They were all given detention for unruly conduct.

There's no way to logically explain the incident anyway, Alex thought miserably.

Furious, Jessica turned on Alex the moment Mr. Heller was gone. "I have never—*never* had detention before! I'll get you for this you . . . you troll!"

"But—" Alex sagged as Jessica marched away, then fell into step beside Robyn and Nicole.

"I *told* you we'd get into trouble," Robyn said.

"So what?" Nicole actually seemed happy because she had to stay an extra hour after school. "Everyone has a right to walk the halls in peace without being tormented."

"Look . . ." Alex paused. "This is all my fault."

"How do you figure that?" Nicole asked.

Good question, Alex thought. She couldn't explain to them why she was responsible, either.

"Jessica was picking on you," Nicole continued. "We heard her. I don't mind being arrested for defending someone's civil rights. Really."

"This is too true," Robyn said with a tolerant

glance at Nicole. "Jessica pulled that stuff out of her locker just to get back at us. You weren't close enough, and neither were we, so nothing else could have happened."

"So we've all got detention on the second day of school. No big deal. We'll have a chance to tell Alex all about our summer vacations," Nicole said.

"I got sunburned so badly I spent most of the time inside while everyone else was out enjoying the beach." Robyn sighed in resignation, then frowned again. "We're gonna be late, Nicole. Come on." Dragging the tall girl away, Robyn looked back. "Catch ya later, Alex!"

"Yeah. Later." Alex waved, then slumped against the wall. It didn't seem right that they were being punished for something she had done. Even if she hadn't meant to do anything wrong, it was her fault they all had detention.

And Jessica would never let her forget it.

CHAPTER 9

Vince and Dave sat in the humvee. They had watched as all the kids were let out from school. Now they watched the stragglers.

From the corner of his eye Vince saw Dave take an apple from the grocery bag and polish it on his shirt. The man had not stopped stuffing his face for the past eight hours.

Vince was looking forward to firing the incompetent boob. Just as soon as this whole mess was behind them and they had found the kid. . . .

He still hoping to avoid a house-to-house

search, which could take days. He hoped they might spot a kid who would trigger a recollection in Dave's feeble mind.

Dave bit into the bright red fruit with a loud crunch, then spoke before he finished chewing. "Except for those girls playing basketball over there, all the kids have gone home."

In one impulsive motion, Vince grabbed the apple and tossed it out the window. "Now," he said calmly, enjoying the distressed expression on Dave's face. "What were you saying?"

"Uh—all the kids have gone home." Wisely, Dave folded his hands in his lap.

"Not quite." Vince picked up the binoculars lying on the seat and handed them to Dave as three girls came through the front doors. "Check them out."

"I've told you over and over, Vince. I didn't get a good look at that kid."

"Check them out anyway." Vince struggled to hold back his temper. He could not stand the thought of having to spend another day in Dave's annoying presence. He wanted that kid now. Danielle was depending on him and, somehow, he would come through for her.

* * *

Alex was just behind Robyn and Nicole as they finally left detention and pushed through the front doors. The girls' basketball team was practicing on the school court.

"Too bad Jessica had to miss practice." Nicole giggled.

"She didn't miss it," Robyn said, pointing. "She's just going to be a little late."

Jessica darted through a side door and ran to the court. Dropping her books on the grass, she immediately joined in the play. Scott was there, too, giving them some pointers.

Intent on watching Scott make a perfect jump shot, Alex almost ran into Nicole when the girl stopped suddenly. There was a large puddle forming on the walk ahead as water poured from a broken lawn sprinkler.

Alex quickly looked away. Her toes began to tingle.

Nicole had not stopped because of the puddle. She pointed at the black vehicle parked across the street. "Careful, girls. Some guy over there is watching us through binoculars."

"Probably an FBI stakeout or something," Robyn whispered ominously.

It isn't the FBI, Alex realized with a gasp. Annie was certain the gold stuff had been manufactured illegally by Paradise Valley Chemical. *Maybe the men in the truck are looking for me!* The tingling in her toes stopped.

"FBI surveillance of a junior high school?" Nicole rolled her eyes. "I don't think so."

Robyn frowned as she studied the black vehicle. "They're from the chemical plant. My dad mentioned something about a truck accident yesterday, but he wouldn't give with the details. Think there's a connection?"

"Probably not," Alex said, "but maybe we should take the long way home." Her worried gaze took in the humvee to her left, the puddle straight ahead, and the basketball team on the right.

Trapped.

"You'd think grown men would have better things to do than spy on innocent kids." Nicole's brow furrowed with indignation, and Alex was afraid she was going to march across the street and tell them exactly that.

Nervous and shaky, Alex glanced at her

hands. She just knew she was going to start to glow any second.

Inside the humvee, the driver snatched the binoculars away from a second man. Then the black vehicle drove away.

Safe for now, Alex thought with a long sigh.

"Catch!" Someone yelled.

Alex, Nicole, and Robyn looked up to see a basketball sail toward them. On the court, Jessica and her friends had stopped playing to watch in eager anticipation.

Alex's ability to move objects engaged without warning. As she concentrated her thoughts on the basketball to deflect it, Scott called out.

"Watch it!"

Alex glanced at him, projecting her thoughts in his direction instead of toward the basketball.

Shock spread across Scott's face as he was suddenly thrown backward onto the ground—struck by an invisible fist.

Appalled by what she had done, Alex stared at him.

The basketball fell from the sky.

Robyn threw her arms over her head and ducked. Nicole dropped her backpack, reached to catch the basketball, and missed. It landed in the puddle, splashing water all over her and the backpack. Nicole froze, then slowly turned to glower at the girls' basketball team.

"Nice catch!" Jessica hurled the taunt with satisfaction. The other girls laughed.

Alex's gaze and thoughts were locked on Scott.

Stunned, he shook his head and looked around for his attacker. No one was standing within five feet of him. Rising, he dusted himself off and approached Alex.

"Look at you guys," he said sympathetically to Nicole. "What a mess!" Scott picked up the backpack and held it out. Water dripped out of the bottom. "I hope your books aren't ruined."

"It's not your fault if they are." Nicole took the soggy bag while continuing to glare at Jessica.

Alex knew where the responsibility lay—squarely on Jessica's shoulders. Alex hadn't meant to collide with the older girl the day before or earlier that morning. She had not intentionally interfered with the girls' basketball practice or made Jessica drop her notebook and lose her homework. And if Jessica hadn't been picking on her, none of them would have gotten detention. But Jessica didn't care. The older girl just didn't like her and was using those unfortunate events as an excuse to torment her.

Alex's gaze narrowed and targeted the girl who was watching her with such amused pleasure. It would be so easy to use her powers to teach Jessica a lesson. So easy . . .

With a single thought, Alex could make her miss every shot. A wave of her hand could discharge an electric jolt that would give the pretty girl a really bad hair day. So easy—and so very, very wrong.

But the suggestion had been planted. Alex's thoughts focused on Jessica.

Then Scott touched her arm. "Are you okay?"

Revenge and Jessica were both forgotten as Alex turned to gaze into Scott's brown eyes.

"Don't worry about Jessica," Scott said. "Sometimes she just gets carried away with herself. You know?"

"Uh-huh," Alex stammered, "yes, yes, I do know. It's okay. Really."

Scott grinned. "That's cool."

Alex was suddenly very glad Scott had distracted her before she had done something terrible to Jessica. The mysterious powers were very precious, and they should not be used for revenge ... or against people in any way. That wouldn't be right.

"Yuck!" Robyn snorted with disgust, drawing Alex's attention to the girl's shoes, which were planted in an inch of water.

Water.

The puddle on the sidewalk suddenly filled Alex's vision and settled in her mind. She shook her head, but she couldn't shake the image. Before she'd been preoccupied with Scott, but now. ... The warm tingling started at her toes and began to work its way through her legs and arms. Panic seized her.

Staring at the puddle, unable to divert her thoughts, Alex stood paralyzed and horror-stricken. She was going to morph into a blob of clear gunk in front of her friends, Jessica, and Scott.

And there was nothing she could do about it.

CHAPTER 10

Oh, no! Alex's knees shook as her molecular structure quickly approached the transformation threshold.

"Come on, Scott!" Jessica walked over and picked up the wet basketball.

Alex fought the process, but her efforts were useless. On the brink of losing it, she desperately wanted her sister.

Annie! Help!

But Annie wasn't there. Alex was alone and helpless—or was she? She remembered what

Annie had suggested that morning. It was worth a try. The worst that could happen was that the distraction technique wouldn't work.

Multiplication tables.

"Two times two is four." Alex's voice wavered with a gurgling quality. "Two times three is six. . . ."

Everyone looked at her like she had suddenly gone bonkers, but Alex didn't care. She'd rather have Scott thinking she was certifiably insane than knowing she could turn into human gelatin.

"Two times four is eight. Two times five is ten. . . ." Imagining a brick wall, solid and sturdy, Alex continued to recite. Her body instantly reverted to its normal, solid, non-tingly state. *Thank you, Annie!*

"What *is* the dweeb doing?" Jessica asked with contempt.

Nicole turned to Jessica. "I'd be surprised if you can *count* to ten."

Raymond sauntered across the lawn toward them, swinging his sax case. He frowned when he caught Alex's worried gaze and edged over to her side. "You okay, Alex?"

Holding her breath, Alex squeezed her arm

just to be sure she was really herself again and safe. Her skin felt warm and the muscle underneath remained firm.

Relieved, she nodded and whispered, "Close call, but I'm all right now."

"First game's in two weeks, Scott," Jessica said impatiently. "Let's go!"

"Yeah, right." Scott turned to follow Jessica, then glanced back at Alex with a puzzled frown.

Alex smiled tightly, then sighed as Scott shook his head and ran toward the court. *So much for making a good impression on Scott.*

Suddenly, Scott looked back and waved. "See ya tomorrow."

Catching her lower lip in her teeth, Alex waved back. Maybe all was not completely lost.

"Come on, Alex. Let's go home. I'm starved." Raymond patted his stomach.

"You're always hungry, Raymond." Alex looked at her other friends, who were watching them expectantly. "But I promised Robyn and Nicole I'd walk with them."

Raymond perked up significantly. Waving the

two girls over, he positioned himself between them, grinned and urged them down the sidewalk.

Now that they're in the seventh grade, maybe Robyn and Nicole qualified as girl-type girls, Alex thought as she walked behind them. Right now, though, she had more important things to worry about than Raymond's social life or even Scott's opinion of her. Men in a black truck from the chemical plant were watching the school.

They were looking for her.

Back home, Alex and Raymond stood outside the garage. Alex took a deep breath, then knocked on the door.

"Who's there?" Annie called from inside.

"It's Alex, Annie. Can Raymond and I come in?"

A long moment passed before Annie replied. "It's open."

Easing in the door, Alex dropped her backpack on the floor and her chin on her chest.

"What's with you, Alex? Your head too heavy for your neck or something?"

Raymond rolled his eyes and walked over to the workbench. Setting down his saxophone case, he moved to the sink and turned on the water.

Alex let the sarcasm pass. She had it coming after the way she had behaved that morning. "I was wrong, Annie . . . about being able to figure out and deal with these powers by myself."

Annie waited without saying anything for a change.

Raymond leaned over to drink from the tap.

"Help!" Alex looked at Annie anxiously.

Annie hesitated, then extended her hand. "Okay, Alex, but you've got to listen to me and cooperate. This is serious."

"I know." Alex felt a hundred times better than she had since the accident. After all, Annie was a genius. If anyone could figure out and teach her to control the bizarre effects of the gold chemical, Annie Mack could.

"I owe you an apology, too, Raymond. I really didn't mean to scare you yesterday."

"Forget it." Raymond straightened and wiped his mouth with his hand. "If you want to know the truth, it was kinda fun." Grinning, he turned around to shut off the water.

Relieved, Alex inhaled deeply. "There's something else you both need to know—"

"Leapin' lizards!" Raymond yelped. "You guys better come look at this."

"What is it?" Alex asked anxiously as she peered past Raymond toward the street. The black humvee with the Paradise Valley Chemical logo painted on its side careened around a curve and sped past the Mack house.

"What does it mean?" Raymond asked.

"Trouble," Annie replied solemnly. "Big trouble."

"That's what I was trying to tell you." Alex sat down on an old, swivel piano stool next to the train table. "Those men were watching the school this afternoon."

Raymond pulled up the milk crate and straddled it. "Think they're looking for you?"

"Who else?"

"Did they see you?" Annie asked.

"Yeah. Through a pair of binoculars. But then they left."

"So maybe they don't know exactly what you

look like." Head bowed in thought, Annie paced. "We've got to play this cool."

"Maybe I should tell Dad what happened," Alex said earnestly. "He can take me to the plant and maybe they can give me an antidote or something."

"No way!" Annie was firm. "My guess is that what doused you is something illegal and extremely top secret. You go public, and Dad could lose his job—or worse."

"Worse?" Alex gasped.

"I'd say Danielle Atron and her security guys never let you see the light of day again." Annie's dark eyes flashed as she stopped before Alex to make her point. "They'll cut you up piece by piece and examine you under a microscope like some frog in biology class!"

Alex's eyes widened with fear. Annie was being more blunt than usual. Alex realized she was in real danger, and not just because the gold stuff had weird side effects, either. Danielle Atron had men out looking for her, and they didn't want to help.

"I'll bet your brain ends up in a jar of formaldehyde," Raymond added with annoying calm.

Annie groaned with disgust. "Ray! Why don't you go see what you can find out about that truck?"

Raymond rose and snapped to attention. "Right." He saluted, then wheeled and marched to the door.

Numb with shock, Alex just stared at the door after it closed behind him.

Espionage was dangerous and very hard on the nerves.

Walking across lawns and ducking behind shrubs and trees, Raymond slowly made his way toward the black humvee he had seen through the garage window. It was parked on the corner, just down the block from Alex's house. Two men were sitting in the front seat. One wore the dark blue cap and lighter blue shirt that meant he was a plant driver. The man behind the steering wheel had short blond hair and just looked mean.

Concealed behind a large tree, Raymond hesitated. He could go back to the garage and report the position of the humvee, but that wouldn't tell Annie anything she didn't already know. Or he could try to get close enough to hear what the two men were talking about. A dangerous task, but the information might save Alex's life, and Alex was the best friend he had.

Raymond sprang onto the sidewalk and ran behind a dark red sedan parked on the street. He kept his eyes trained on the humvee. The driver seemed to be studying a map, and the other man was staring out the windshield and hadn't noticed him—yet. Raymond darted along the side of the car.

Best to just keep moving. Ignoring his pounding heart and wobbly knees, he ran for the back of the humvee and hunkered down. The windows were open, and he could hear the men's conversation clearly. Raymond chanced a peek through the back window. The mean-looking driver was speaking.

"We do this block, then another three. I want to cover the whole neighborhood by nightfall."

"Don't worry," said a softer voice. "Even if I don't recognize the kid, he'll probably recognize me."

Raymond blinked and scratched his head. *What a dumb thing to say.* Having Alex recognize the guys who were looking for her wouldn't help them at all. It would warn Alex. He heard the first man sigh wearily. Apparently he thought it was dumb, too.

"All we need is the right kid to slip his hand in this handprint ID unit," said the driver, "and we'll nail him."

Raymond inhaled softly. He didn't know exactly what a handprint ID unit was, but it would identify Alex. And he had to warn her.

Suddenly, the driver opened his door.

Raymond flattened himself against the back of the humvee and froze.

"Let's go," the driver ordered. He got out and slammed the door.

Raymond held his breath as the passenger door opened and slammed shut. The other man started walking toward the back of the humvee.

"This way!" The mean man snapped impatiently.

"Right." The other man moved forward again.

Raymond waited a minute, then peeked

around the side of the truck. The two men were walking toward the nearest house with their backs to him. One of them carried a metal container the size of a shoebox. Ray didn't waste another second, but dashed for the opposite sidewalk and raced back to Annie and Alex.

CHAPTER 11

Alex knew something bad was happening the minute Raymond burst into the garage. "What's wrong?"

"Those guys are plant security!" Raymond paced back and forth with nervous excitement. "They're going door-to-door. They have something you stick your hand in that identifies you! You're in big trouble." Raymond paused and fixed Alex with a worried stare.

Panic seized Alex and sent her thoughts into turmoil. Electrical devices all over the garage turned on and off. The weed trimmer whirred. The model train raced along the tracks. The lights blazed and dimmed.

"Alex, you're glowing!" Annie took her hand. "You've got to get hold of yourself."

"I can't!" Alex jerked free and ran to the mirror. Her face shone with golden light. "If they see me like this, I'm dead!"

Annie remained calm and cool, which helped settle Alex's jangled nerves.

"You have to calm down," Annie said. "Then you'll stop glowing. Okay?"

Nodding, Alex didn't protest when Annie took her arm and pushed her toward the door that led to the kitchen.

Annie opened the door, then instantly closed it again. "Mom's in there."

"I can't let her see me like this!" Alex wailed.

"I know. She just finished mopping the floor. Maybe she'll leave in a minute. You just need a little time to compose yourself. Now, take a deep breath—"

"Well, you can forget that!" Raymond was still in spy-mode, looking out the window through narrowed eyes, on the alert for any signs of trouble. "We're out of time. They're heading for this house right now."

Alex's heart zoomed into her throat and she shivered with fear. Her glowing skin brightened. She did not want to end up on a lab table at Paradise Valley Chemical. Going through junior high as a notorious dweeb seemed infinitely more appealing than being a freak in the clutches of Danielle Atron.

Alex could almost see the wheels turning in Annie's head as she quietly opened the door again. She closed it even faster than the first time.

"What?" Alex asked.

"Now she's sorting the laundry." Annie paused with her hand on her chin to consider the problem.

"Laundry!" The golden glow intensified as Alex glanced at the washer and dryer. There was no place to run or hide. The plant security men were outside, and her mother was blocking the only way from the garage to the house. She needed to spend a few minutes someplace where she felt safe or she wouldn't be able to stop glowing. "She can't do the laundry now!"

"Alex, you're going to have to liquefy."

Alex balked. Annie had no idea how weird and scary it was to feel your body changing into a fluid on a molecular level. Besides, she had only morphed by accident. She didn't know if she could transform on command whenever she felt like it.

"What if I can't?"

Annie tried to bolster Alex's confidence. "You can do it."

"You've got only two choices, Alex." Raymond looked over his shoulder, then stepped away from the window. "Turn into a puddle or spend the rest of your life as Danielle Atron's pet lab rat."

"Go home, Raymond," Annie commanded. "And when they come to your house, try not to say anything too stupid."

Insulted, Raymond scowled at Annie as he slid between the two girls and left.

Alex sympathized with Raymond, but she would have to apologize for Annie later. Right now, she was too terrified to worry about it.

Annie stepped back. "Ready?"

Alex nodded. All she could do was try.

"Go for it."

Water, Alex thought, concentrating on the bottle of water that had planted the suggestion in her mind yesterday. A tingling sensation began to spread throughout her body, and her skin prickled. *Water, water, water* . . . Her cells shifted into a stiff gel, then into a thick liquid state. Alex was suddenly on the floor—a puddle.

"Now what?" Alex gurgled. She was getting the hang of speaking clearly, despite being a puddle.

Annie glanced at the sink. "You're gonna have to go through the plumbing."

"Plumbing! No way!"

"You've got no choice," Annie insisted. "You've got to get past Mom and upstairs so you can calm down. I'll stall those security guys until you stop glowing. Go on!"

Annie's head snapped around when the doorbell rang. She sprang for the door.

Alone, liquified, and scared, Alex wailed. "Is that all you're going to say to me?"

Annie looked back with a weak smile. "Good luck." Then she was gone through the door.

117

Annie was right, Alex realized as she oozed up the side of the sink. She didn't have a choice. Alex poured herself down the drain.

Annie hurried past her mom as she set down the laundry basket and moved to go answer the door. "I'll get it."

But Mr. Mack had opened the front door moments before Annie arrived. "Oh, Annie." He stepped aside to make room for her. "This is Vince and Dave. They're from the plant, and they just want to ask you a couple of questions."

Annie steeled herself to be interrogated and wondered how Alex was doing.

The pipes were dark, cold, and damp. Alex started out slowly, trying to orient herself in the confusing maze of hollow metal. With no map to follow, she decided the best route was through the kitchen to the downstairs bathroom, then straight up to the second floor. She'd feel safe in her bedroom.

Flowing easily, she entered the kitchen pipes. She could hear her mother humming. The sound reassured her, and Alex detoured into the curved pipe under the kitchen sink. *Hmmm. There's a clog here. I'll have to tell Dad. . . .* Her mom walked over to the sink and stood right above her, lifting something.

A bucket!

Too late, Alex realized how foolish she had been to hesitate. A rush of water charged her as Mrs. Mack dumped the contents of the bucket, washing Alex back the way she had come. *Yuck! Gross!* Alex yelped as the dirty water hit her.

Fighting the powerful tide, she expanded and lodged herself within the pipe. Her backward movement was halted, and after letting the mop water seep by her, she hurried on toward the bathroom.

She did not make any more stops. There would be plenty of time to experiment with her strange liquid form later, but only if plant security didn't find out Alex Mack was the kid they were looking for.

Annie took stock of the enemy.

Dave was holding a metal box, which had to be the handprint ID unit. He looked distracted, confused, and uneasy. Annie got the impression that he had to refer to a manual in order to tie his shoes every morning.

Vince was a different matter. With close-cropped blond hair, cold blue eyes, and a rigid expression, there was no question that the man was confident, intelligent, and dangerous. His icy stare bore straight through her.

"Sweetheart," Vince said with phony pleasantness. "Do you know where you were at three-thirty yesterday afternoon?"

Vince's tight, insincere grin chilled Annie to the bone, but she refused to be intimidated. "Sweetheart?" Her tone dripped with sarcasm. "I don't even know you."

Dave popped a chocolate candy in his mouth and shifted awkwardly from one foot to the other. A second candy followed the first before he was finished chewing, and he moved a step back so Vince wouldn't notice.

Vince maintained his smile with difficulty, his attention riveted on Annie. "I apologize."

"At three-thirty, I was in my advanced placement chemistry class working on a gravity waves experiment."

Nodding, but not necessarily convinced, Vince

looked back at Mr. Mack. "And your other daughter?"

"She had basketball tryouts yesterday." Mr. Mack glanced at Annie. "Right?"

"Right."

Suddenly interested, Vince looked pointedly at Dave. The driver stopped chewing until Vince's gaze was once again fastened on Mr. Mack and Annie. "And where is she now?"

"I haven't seen her this afternoon," Mr. Mack said.

"She's upstairs, Dad."

Vince moved forward with Dave close behind. "Why don't we go check on that?"

Annie's pulse increased sharply. How was she going to keep them out of the house long enough for Alex to stop glowing like a neon sign?

"Wait just a second, guys," Mr. Mack said firmly. "She's my daughter. I'll bring her down."

Startled, Annie watched as her easygoing father stood up to the strong-arm of Paradise Valley Chemical. She had never been more proud of him.

Annie quickly closed the door in Vince's face, relishing the taste of minor victory as her father left to find Alex. She only hoped that when he did, Alex would look like Alex and not a giant glob of glowing Jell-O.

Alex stopped when the pipe she was traveling through split in two. The plumbing network in the house was a confusing labyrinth of turns and junctions, and she quivered with indecision and anxiety.

She was hopelessly lost.

CHAPTER 12

Alex zipped into the pipe on the right. She didn't know where she'd find herself at the end of her unusual trek, but at least she'd be on the second floor.

A spot of light shining through a drain appeared ahead. Alex bolted for it and emerged in the tub of the bathroom she shared with Annie. She didn't waste time trying to materialize on the spot, but flowed under the closed door into the hall.

The unmistakable thud of footsteps sounded on the stairs.

Alex glided under her bedroom door and re-formed. Relief washed over her as she turned to look in the mirror. She wasn't glowing. Trying to get through the pipes safely had taken her mind off her other fears. The gentle sound of her father's voice reinforced her sense of calm. He wouldn't let anything terrible happen to her.

"Alex?" Her father called from the hallway.

Perching on the edge of her bed, Alex leaned over and grabbed a book lying on the floor. The title was *Atom*, Annie's physics text. Alex hoped her father wouldn't notice.

She opened the book, realized it was upside down, and turned it right-side up just as her father opened the door and looked in.

"Alex. Well, here you are." Mr. Mack sounded surprised. "I didn't see you come in."

Forcing a bright smile, Alex tried to respond casually. "I yelled 'hi.' I thought you heard me."

"Do you know anything about an accident near school yesterday?"

"An accident?" Alex's brain stalled for a moment, then she shrugged and forced another smile. "Nope."

"Good." Mr. Mack seemed relieved and

shoved his hands in his pockets. "I need you to come downstairs and tell a couple of people that."

"Sure."

Mr. Mack stepped aside to let Alex walk in front of him. All the way down the hall, then down the staircase, he kept a comforting hand on her shoulder.

Alex stopped suddenly on the bottom stair, almost tripping her father. She felt panicky. What if she couldn't control herself and turned into a puddle or started to glow again?

"This isn't anything to worry about, Alex," Mr. Mack said gently. "Just tell them you don't know anything and that'll be the end of it."

Her father's concern helped Alex stay calm. Nodding, she eased through the door as Annie opened it. Annie moved in beside her, and Mr. Mack stood protectively behind both of them.

Alex instantly recognized the man who had crashed the truck. She looked at the other one.

"Here she is, Vince," Mr. Mack said evenly. "My younger daughter, Alex."

"I was upstairs doing my homework," Alex added for good measure. Her voice shook a little, but she made herself look Vince in the eye as he studied her suspiciously.

"Did you make the team?" Vince asked pointedly.

Team? Alex didn't have any idea what he was talking about. Then she remembered that Annie had used basketball tryouts to explain her absence to her father yesterday.

"No," she said, trying to sound disappointed.

"But you saw the accident." Vince phrased his words as a statement, not a question.

"What accident?" Alex asked innocently. She looked straight at Vince. He glared back suspiciously.

"That should do it, gentlemen." Mr. Mack smiled at Alex, then tried to dismiss the security men. "So if you don't mind, we'd like to eat our dinner.'

"As soon as they have their handprints recorded," Vince said coldly. "So we know they've been checked out."

The man holding the metal box—Dave, according to the patch on his blue shirt—stepped forward and extended the device.

Alex stared at the opening in one end of the

long box. She knew she couldn't put her hand in there. If she did, they'd know she was the kid at the scene of the accident. And if she panicked now, she'd start to glow again.

Just then, Annie stepped forward and Mr. Mack nodded for her to go ahead of Alex. Obviously nervous, Annie slowly inserted her hand into the box.

Even though Annie knows she isn't the kid they're looking for, she's frightened, too. Suddenly Alex understood why. It was wrong for a plant operation to have an illegal chemical, threaten the neighborhood, and track down an innocent kid. *Danielle Atron and her henchmen shouldn't be allowed to get away with it. It just isn't fair,* Alex thought.

A greenish yellow light was visible through the opening as the high-tech gadget read and compared Annie's handprint to the one on file.

No match.

Removing her hand, Annie regarded Alex anxiously.

Alex stared at the box, her thoughts racing. *What am I going to do?*

As she moved her hand toward the opening,

she concentrated on the box. Images of the box flying through the air filled her mind. Just as her fingers touched the metal rim, Dave jerked, and the device flipped out of his grasp. It landed on the walkway and broke into several pieces, revealing a black file print on a white background surrounded by small, electronic components.

"Oh, no!" Dave moaned. He instantly turned to Vince. "I'm sorry, Vince, but we have another one in the car."

Not for long, Alex thought. Concentrating on the black humvee parked on the street, Alex visualized the brake pedal and the gear shift. With the force of her own thoughts, she moved the gear lever into neutral, then released the brake. The humvee began to roll.

"Excuse me," Annie said. "Isn't that your vehicle rolling away?"

Alex stiffled a giggle as Vince's eyes widened in disbelief. He and Dave turned simultaneously and ran down the walk. Angry and frantic, Vince shoved Dave out of his way as he raced to try and save the runaway humvee. Dave landed on the lawn, but picked himself up and gave chase again. The sound of a loud crash was all the evidence Alex needed to know that the black vehicle and the other ID device would no longer be a problem.

Mr. Mack frowned. "I hope those guys have car insurance."

"I hope they have life insurance," Annie said with a grin. "They'll need it when Danielle gets hold of them."

"Yeah." Laughing, Alex followed Annie inside.

Sitting on the edge of her bed, Alex watched as Annie crossed to her own bed and sat down. They hadn't had a chance to talk alone since dinner.

"I'm worried, Annie. The plant won't stop till they find me."

Annie picked up her alarm clock to set it. "Between my brains and your powers, that won't be so easy." Setting down the clock, Annie squeezed Alex's hands. "Everything's changed, Alex. You were just this average kid, headed for a life of inconsequence and boredom, and now look at you."

Grinning, Alex nodded. No one could ever say she was just plain, old, ordinary Alex Mack again. Then she realized that wasn't quite right. They could say it because no one except Annie and Raymond knew about her amazing new abilities. But she'd at least have the satisfaction of knowing it wasn't true. Alex fell back on her pillow and propped her head on her hand.

Annie leaned back, too, and slipped under the covers. "I'll bet we make the cover of *Scientific American*."

"You would have by yourself eventually."

"Don't worry," Annie said emphatically. "I'll take most of the credit. Good night, Alex." She switched off the lamp on her nightstand.

"Good night, Annie." Pulling her blanket up to her chin, Alex realized that her lamp was on. She was about to sit up, then changed her mind and reached out her hand. An electric jolt sprang from her fingers, shutting the lamp off. Then both lamps began to turn on and off repeatedly.

"Alex!" Annie squealed.

They dissolved into fits of giggles, but a flickering outside drew Alex's curious gaze. Sitting up, she peered out the window. Car alarms blared, dogs barked, and every light on every house and every lamppost within sight was blinking on and off.

Alex snuggled back under the covers and smiled, content in the knowledge that she, Alex Mack, was certainly not boring anymore.

About the Author

Diana G. Gallagher lives in California with her daughter, Chelsea, her best friend, Betsey, three dogs, and five cats. Her grown son, Jay, lives in Kansas. When she's not writing, she likes to read, work in the garden, and walk the dogs. A Hugo Award–winning illustrator, she is best known for her series *Woof: The House Dragon*. Her songs about humanity's future in space are sung at science-fiction conventions throughout the world and have been recorded in cassette form: "Cosmic Concepts More Complete," "Star*Song," and "Fire Dream." Her first novel, *The Alien Dark*, appeared in 1990. She is the author of the forthcoming novel *Star Trek: Deep Space Nine: Arcade*, for young readers. She is working on the next story about *The Secret World of Alex Mack*.